BOTTLED UP

a novel

JAYE MURRAY

Dial Books
New York

Published by Dial Books
A member of Penguin Group (USA) Inc.
345 Hudson Street
New York, New York 10014
Copyright © 2003 by Jaye Murray
All rights reserved
Designed by Lily Malcom
Text set in Meridien
Printed in the U.S.A. on acid-free paper
10 9 8 7 6 5 4 3 2 1
Library of Congress Cataloging-in-Publication Data
Murray, Jaye.
Bottled up / Jaye Murray.
p. cm.
Summary: A high school boy comes to terms with
his drug addiction, life with an alcoholic father, and
a younger brother who looks up to him.
ISBN 0-8037-2897-2
[1. Brothers—Fiction. 2. Family problems—Fiction.
3. Alcoholism—Fiction. 4. Drug abuse—Fiction.
5. High schools—Fiction. 6. Schools—Fiction.]
I. Title.
PZ7.M9615 Bo 2003
[Fic]—dc21
2002013744

"The door's open and we should be able to walk straight through it into the last days without having to count them. What can stop us now?"

This book is dedicated to
Richard Peck
for holding open the door
and giving me every reason
to believe I could go through it.

"And still I'm not through with all I've got to say. I haven't even gotten a good start."

—quotes from *Father Figure* by Richard Peck

BOTTLED UP

ONE

I remember when all I wanted was a ten-speed and a six-pack of Hershey bars.

Now all I want is to be left alone.

"Mr. Downs, I've had it with you."

That's what my teacher Ms. Fleming told me in front of my whole class, and that's how all this started. At least that's my story anyway. You see, I was just going along the same as I always do—then Fleming changed the rules.

I cut fifth period English a lot. But when I don't, I go right to my desk three rows back, get my arm across the top, set my head inside my elbow, and take a nap. I don't snore. I don't bother anybody. Fleming does her thing. I do mine. Nobody gets hassled.

This was working for me. I figured it was working for her

too. Then, out of nowhere, she goes batty with the *I've had it with you* garbage.

I was asleep. I was so deep into some dream, I could have been drooling on my sleeve. Then I felt something pecking at my head. Fleming was slamming her nail into my skull like I was friggin' roadkill and she was a crow going at my brains for lunch.

"Hey, I was sleeping."

"I've really had it with you, Mr. Downs."

With the back of my hand, I wiped off the spit she'd sprayed on my face.

"Go to the principal's office," she said as if she couldn't look at my mug another second without blowing chunks on my desk.

"I wasn't doing anything."

"Exactly. Having you in class is like having a corpse in the third row."

"So let the dead sleep."

"Get out. Go to Mr. Giraldi's office. Maybe he can give you a pillow and send for room service."

"Now we're talkin'," I said, and stood up.

"You don't have any idea what we're talking about in this class. You don't even know who Charles Dickens is."

I didn't really care.

Fleming had her arms crossed. She was trying to get all in my face. She was so close, I could have bitten her fat banana nose off.

I grabbed my never-been-used-before seven-month-old notebook, good for carrying into any class, and started walking.

In the front row Jenna was looking at me. She's one of the good girls—the high-honor-roll, never-get-into-trouble untouchables. She's really not my kind of girl—most of them have tattoos or nose rings—but there's something about her smile. She smiles like she's in love with whoever she's looking at.

She smiled at me a few months ago. I've been trying to get her to do it again ever since.

I stopped at the door. I was going to let loose and tell Fleming where she could stick her Dickens.

"Go to the principal," she said before I could open my mouth. "You're wasting too much of my time, sir."

People love to call a guy *sir* when they really mean *asshole*.

She rushed up to the front of the room to speed me out the door.

"I'm going," I said.

"Not fast enough," she shot back, and shut the door pretty hard in my face.

I thought about my choices. I had two.

I could go to Giraldi's office and listen to him give me hell.

Or—smoke a bone behind the deli across the street.

Some choices are easy.

Fleming could make rules. But I didn't have to follow them.

I want to get myself real high. I want to get so far off the ground that my hair gets caught on cloud dust.

Cloud dust is that stuff clouds leave behind when they're floating real fast across the sky.

That's what I want.

Cloud dust.

■ ■ ■

When Fleming shut that door in my face, she gave me a free period. Free period means that I'm the teacher. I run my own classes:

Pot Smoking 101
Joint Rolling 102 (bring your own spit and paper)
To Hell with Everybody 201 (must have passed 101 first)

I never even thought about going to Giraldi's office. Why should I? Most of the time when a teacher sends me to the principal and I don't show, the teacher doesn't check up on it later. And if I do get busted for not showing, all I get is a detention. Sometimes I show for that, but sometimes I don't. It's all part of the rules—how things have always been.

So I walked right past Giraldi's office, went outside, and lit a Marlboro by the front door. I had it half smoked when I got across the street to the Dumpster behind the deli.

I sat on a milk crate that smelled like cottage cheese, took a tightly rolled joint out of my sock, and struck a match. I watched the tip glow then flake into ash when I inhaled.

Held it.

Exhaled.

I always feel like I'm walking around holding my breath. But when I light up and smoke some weed, it's like I'm breathing for the first time.

Pot smells like nothing else my nose knows. My nostrils hug the smoke, and it goes into my throat that's open like a hungry bird waiting for a worm. I suck in on the joint and hold it. My chest gets so tight, I feel like Superman all puffed out and ready to fly.

Then I let the smoke out real slow. It covers my clothes like it's trying to hide me.

Breathe in.

Hold it.

Hold it.

"Chimney Boy, how the hell are you?"

It was Tony. I blew out the smoke and turned my head his way. Tony works in the deli making sandwiches for the kids at school and slicing meat for old ladies. Good ol' Tony. He never puts enough roast beef on your wedge. It's always lettuce and tomato with a little bit of meat drowning in chunky mayonnaise.

The first time he caught me blowing smoke next to the Dumpster, he just put out his hand for my weed, took a hit, and went back inside. He didn't give me any crap for being there. Now every time he sees me getting high between classes, he has to grub off of me and get his spit all over my blunt.

"How you doing, Tony?"

"Just wasting another damn day, kid. Another day of feeding everybody else while I go hungry." He took my joint and helped himself to two long hits.

"They don't give you anything to eat in there?" I asked him.

"I can eat anything I want. I'm just hungry."

Tony doesn't make a lot of sense, but he never stays long. He comes out, makes a couple of wisecracks about me being a chimney, steals a hit or two, and goes back to work. Fair deal, I guess. Sometimes when I go in for a sandwich, I even get a few extra slabs of meat on my wedge.

I finished off the joint, lit a Marlboro, and wiped off the ashes that had fallen on my tie-dyed T-shirt. That day I was wearing the one that's got three different greens with a swirl of blue in the middle. I have a load of tie-dyed shirts—long-sleeved, short-sleeved, sleeveless, and even a pair of psychedelic purple tie-dyed boxers.

I don't have a favorite color. That's why tie-dye works for me. All the colors mixed up and crazy.

No two tie-dyed anythings are the same.

I want back all the time gym classes ever stole from me.

That's a lot of time when you think about it. Forty-five minutes a few times a week for thirteen years.

I figured it out once. Thirteen years times forty weeks a year, three times a week. Then multiply that by forty-five minutes and it comes out to having crapped away about 20,200 minutes of my life.

Twenty thousand two hundred minutes of throwing dodge balls and doing sit-ups, jumping jacks, squat thrusts, and foul shots. Twenty thousand two hundred minutes of physical "education."

I want my time back.

I showed up ten minutes late for gym class—right on time for me.

Everybody was out of the locker room and in their shorts or sweats. The guys were doing sit-ups and counting out loud like it was damn boot camp.

I used to be into sports when I was a kid. I know all the rules. The one who hits the farthest, gets the most baskets, scores the most goals is king of the who-gives-a-shit hill.

Boys playing with their balls is all that's about.

I got better things to do with mine, like scratch them. At least there's a point to doing that.

The metal bar on the gym door clicked shut behind me.

"Downs," Coach Fredericks yelled over to me. He thinks he's a tough guy, that coach. Big man around the teenage boys. He walks from one side of the gym to the other with a whistle around his neck and one hand going up and down his arm like he's feeling around for a muscle. He calls everybody by their last name. Calls you *Miss* if you screw up a foul shot. Throws volleyballs at your head if you're not listening to him.

"Downs, the principal is waiting for you in his office. What did you do this time?"

"I think it's something about his mother," I said, not looking over at him. "She wants to go out with me again—I don't know."

I pulled myself up onto the sixth step of the bleachers. I was getting ready to do my Invisible Man trick and finish my nap.

Fredericks blew the whistle. "Downs."

"What?" I was on my back with my hands behind my head. My kind of sit-up—lie down and stay down 'til lunch.

"Mr. Giraldi wants you in his office now." He blew the whistle even harder. "Get moving. He probably wants to give you that student of the year award."

"Yeah. Maybe." My eyes were closed and I was hoping he'd just get lost.

But he got louder. "Downs!"

A basketball slammed into the bleacher next to my head.

"Move it!" he was yelling at me. "Don't keep the principal waiting."

"Screw him," I said to myself. Or I *thought* I'd said it to myself, but I guess after all the weed I smoked, by sixth period I didn't know what was coming out of my mouth or how loud.

"If that's what you want to do, Downs. But you may have to buy him dinner or bring him flowers first."

He wasn't going to let up. Most of the guys on the floor were still doing sit-ups, but some of them had fallen back holding their stomachs. They all looked pretty stupid to me with sweat dripping off their heads. They should be like me—forget all this phys. ed. crap and chill out.

That would never happen in my almost-middle-class school of suck-ups. Nobody's got any guts in my high school.

I stood up, got a good stretch with one hand on my butt and the other over my head.

"Sometime today, burnout," one of the guys yelled from the floor.

I jumped off the bleachers and looked to see which idiot wanted my foot up his ass. No one said anything else. Like I said—none of these guys have any guts.

"Get out of my gym, Downs." Fredericks pointed to the door. I walked over to it and pushed it open with my butt. The metal rod on the door rattled when it slammed shut behind me.

I heard Fredericks still yelling at me. "Don't forget to bring Giraldi some flowers."

Yeah, bite me.

I remember my father asking me, back when I was eight, why I didn't like the name Phillip.

"It's dumb," was all I told him.

"Pip's any better?" he asked.

I said something like, Duh.

"That's okay," he said. "Maybe you're just a Pip off the old block."

I wasn't sure what he meant by that, but I remember hoping he was wrong.

■ ■ ■

When I got out of the gym Giraldi was stomping down the hall at me.

"Let's go, mister." He turned right around on his heel like some military dude and stomped back the other way again.

I took my time.

"I told you to move it, Phillip."

I stopped. "My name is Pip." I shoved my hands in the pockets of my jeans and figured if he couldn't get this much straight we had no place to go.

Nobody calls me Phillip. Nobody.

"Maybe you should stick to being called Phillip instead of answering to a dog's name. Or maybe we should start calling you Pup instead."

Or maybe he should shut the hell up.

Nobody would believe me if I told them my principal talks like this. Nobody would believe Fleming was poking at me with her nail either, or that the coach tossed a basketball right next to my head.

That's all right. People wouldn't believe half the crap *I* pull either.

He could call me a dog if he wanted to, he just couldn't call me Phillip. That's one of *my* rules.

"Come on, Pup," Giraldi said, heading for his office. "And tie your shoelaces."

"Why?"

"You're going to fall—trip and break your neck."

"What do you care?"

He looked past me for a second, then behind him like he was looking for his answer.

"I don't want you scuffing my floors. Tie your shoes."

I stopped and bent down like I was going to tie them. As

soon as he turned around to stomp off, I stood up and left my shoes the way I like them. Untied.

He had to hear my laces hitting the floor. I know he did. I was letting them slap hard.

He slowed down when we were almost to the main office. I figured he was going to tell me to tie them again.

"We need to have a man-to-man talk," he said with this serious look on his face.

"Or man-to-dog," I told him.

He stopped at the door with his hand on the knob and looked at me. For a second he didn't look like a principal—not like forty-something-year-old Giraldi, who's waiting on his pension. He looked like a person. Or maybe he was looking at *me* like *I* was a person. But that only lasted a second.

"I don't understand you," he said, looking over my head, then back at me again. "Why would you want to spend the rest of your life being an uneducated, drug-taking wiseass?"

"What are you talking about?" I put on my best *I'm confused* look. "I'm not a wiseass."

He rolled his eyes and opened the door. "That's all you can say?" he asked, stepping into his office.

I answered him the only way I knew how.

"Woof."

I remember this one time when my father took me out for ice cream.

After the second lick off my strawberry cone, the scoop fell right onto my shoe.

I stood there holding the empty cone in my hand and watched my father lick his ice cream.

After a minute of me doing nothing to help myself, he handed me his cone and took mine. Then he bent over, picked the scoop off my shoe, and shoved it on top.

He ate that one.

Giraldi sits right down at his desk and tells me, "Shut the door."

So I shut it.

"Sit," he says.

Shut the door, sit, roll over, play dead.

I plop into my regular chair right across from him. I've sat there so many times, I think my butt is making its own groove. I stretch out my legs in front of me and let my laces slap on the floor again.

"Ms. Fleming sent you to my office last period and you didn't show. Why not?"

"I came by but you weren't here."

"You didn't wait."

"I had to study. I went to the library."

"You've never stepped foot into the school library."

I stared at a spot right behind him. I wasn't really looking at anything. I just picked a spot, stared, and blocked him out. I didn't even blink or move my face or nothin'. I acted like I couldn't hear a word he was saying.

He moved some papers around on his desk. I figured it was my file. It always comes back to my file with Giraldi.

"I've got more disciplinary forms on you than anyone else has ever gotten in the history of this school."

How the hell would he know that?

"You ever going to get a haircut?" he asked me, like he figures if I'd just tie my shoes and keep my hair short, I wouldn't end up in his office.

"If you're so desperate to play dress up," I said, "why don't you get yourself a friggin' Barbie doll?"

I went back to staring in front of me. I wasn't listening to him anymore. He was going on about how he was sick of me, tired of wasting his time—same old stuff.

Then he said, "No detentions. No suspension. No long talk. You're out of here."

He moved some more papers, then I heard him lift the phone receiver.

I still didn't look, because I'm too cool for that.

He dialed, then waited.

"May I speak with Mr. Michael Downs, please? Yes. I'll hold."

My head snapped from where I was staring. He could see the *oh crap* look in my eyes.

He didn't blink.

I jumped up out of my seat. "What the hell are you doing?" My heart was pounding so hard under my shirt, it made my armpit hurt.

"I'm calling your father to let him know you're being expelled and to recommend some good rehab programs."

I reached across the desk and slammed my finger on the phone button.

"What do you think you're doing?" he asked me with the receiver still in his hand. I've pulled a lot of crap, but hanging up his phone was a new one.

I just stared at him. I blew the hair out of my eyes and watched to see if he was going to dial the phone again.

"Sit back down," he said. I couldn't move. I was stuck in that spot and I needed to be close enough to click the phone again if he dialed.

He was staring at me. Hard. Not like he was mad, though. It was the way he looked at me outside in the hall—like I was a person. And he saw something. He must have, because he put the receiver back down.

"Sit," he repeated.

I sat, but on the edge of the seat. I was ready to jump up at any time. I didn't go back to staring at the spot behind him. I looked right at his face. I'd never noticed that the guy had green eyes.

"I have no choice but to expel you. You cause more trouble than anyone else, and you take up too much of my time and your teachers'. I can't keep chasing you, talking to you, trying to get you to shape up. You're beyond help—my help, anyway. I have enough disciplinary forms here to wallpaper my office."

"You can't." I think my voice even cracked then. I'm sure I sounded like an idiot.

"Tell me one reason why not."

I nodded toward the newspaper on his desk next to the phone.

"You read the paper?" I asked him.

"Yes. Why?"

"You call my father, tell him I'm expelled, and you'll be reading about me on the front page tomorrow."

"I don't understand."

"Father Kills Teen Son—"

"Phillip—"

"You don't get it." My voice was shaking. "You make that call and I'm a dead man."

He sat back in his chair, picked a pen up off the desk, and started twisting it. We sat there for I don't know how many minutes.

I waited. What else could I do? Waiting him out was my only shot.

He finally spoke up. "I said before that you were beyond my help. Now I'm thinking that maybe there is one other choice we have. I'm thinking that you need someone to talk to. With the right guidance maybe you can learn to use the brain you've got hidden under all that hair."

He pulled a little white card out of his desk and handed it to me. "Call her by the end of the day. Have an appointment set up for tomorrow and I'll hold off speaking to your father."

It was a business card: *Claire Butler—Jensen Family Counseling Center.*

"I don't need counseling." I put the card back on his desk.

"Just your saying that to me is proof of how badly you need it. This is your only ticket off the front page of the paper and you're not even giving it a moment's thought."

He shook his head and kept talking. "You need to learn that the things you do and don't do have repercussions. If you're this afraid of your father, you should stop getting into so much trouble and make some right choices. Start with this one."

"I don't have any money for counseling."

"It won't cost you money."

He was holding the card out for me. I took it from him.

"Your parents don't have to know you're going. The services are confidential."

I shoved the card in my back pocket.

"Make the right choice. Go to counseling and attend all your classes or I'll expel you. According to your story, that means you die. Sounds like a no-brainer to me."

All I wanted to do was get out of there. I needed a joint. I needed to smoke Giraldi out—blow all this up into the air.

I needed a bone. I needed it bad.

Fetch.

I want to be six years old again—just for a day.
It's not that things were so much better back then. They sucked.
But I was the kind of kid who knew how to laugh about it all.
That's what I want. I want to laugh.

My brother's name is Mikey—Michael Downs, Jr., really. But I call him Bugs because that's what he does to me.

People say I've got an answer for everything. I don't think so. But my little brother has a *question* for everything.

Why do they call them Band-Aids and not Cut-Covers?

Why does Ronald McDonald have a white face?

Do the Yankees wear blue-pinstriped pajamas?

And he has eight million questions about everything you'd never need to know about M&M's.

How do they get the shells around the chocolate?

How do they know which ones are supposed to be yellow and which ones are supposed to be green?

I almost always give him the same answer.

Shut up, I tell him.

He's got a whole load of questions about our family too. Same answer.

Shut up.

After getting rattled by Giraldi and having to sit through the rest of my classes without a buzz, all I wanted to do was smoke a joint. I wasn't in the mood for a pain-in-the-butt six-year-old and his stupid questions. I just wanted to kick back and forget things for a little while.

He was standing next to a tree in front of the school, looking at his hand.

"Let's go," I said.

"Look at this." He put the back of his hand in front of his face.

"It's a ladybug," I told the little genius. "You've seen a million of those."

"Not like this one. This one doesn't have any spots."

"Let's get out of here."

"I'm naming her No Spots."

He was just standing there, not listening to me. I should call him No Ears.

"Come on." I grabbed the top of his shirt and pulled him to start walking.

"Look over there," he said, pointing with his other hand behind him at a yellow backhoe and a dump truck. "They started digging today. I think they're fixing something. Cool, right?"

I pulled on his shirt a little harder and got him crossing the street.

"Stop," he yelled, and bent down to the double yellow line, feeling around with his hands. "I dropped her."

"Who?"

"No Spots."

The light turned green and a car honked at us. I gave the lady a good look at my middle finger, and pulled my brother across the street.

"She'll get squished," he yelled at me.

"Forget the bug, *we're* going to get flattened." I pulled him the rest of the way across the street. "You couldn't find her because she probably flew away."

His Superman backpack was falling off his shoulders and I yanked it up when we got to the sidewalk.

"Pip? Why do ladybugs fly?"

"Because their legs are too small to walk on all day."

"They got a lot of places to go?"

"Maybe."

"God gave them wings so they wouldn't get tired?"

"I don't know about God."

"So how'd they get wings?"

"Could you just shut up and walk?" I needed a joint more than I needed to breathe. I felt like some extra layer of skin was growing on me and the only way to lose it was to get stoned. I pulled a pack of Marlboros out of the front of my jeans and shook out a cigarette.

"Pip? Are you taking me to Eddie's house again?"

"Yeah. His mother is gonna watch you for a little while."

I lit the butt and took a breath in.

"How come you don't take me home anymore?" He was whining. "I'm sick of going to Eddie's house. You're supposed to pick me up and take me home."

I blew out the smoke. "Eddie's your friend. You two can hang out—"

"I want to hang out with *you.*"

"You can't."

"Where are you going?"

"Nowhere."

"So why can't I come?"

"Shut up, Bugs."

The kid was mad at me. He was sick of getting dumped off,

but I didn't care. I wanted to finish that one joint I had in my sock, even though it wasn't going to be enough to un-rattle me.

I took a long drag on my cigarette.

"Can I try that?"

"Try what? My cigarette?"

"Uh-huh."

"No way."

"Why not?"

I squatted down and blew smoke into his face. He started coughing and waved his hands to push it away.

Sometimes I wonder who Mikey's going to be in ten years. I could really come up with some ideas around that, but none of them would be good. Crap. I don't need any of it on my head, that's for sure. There was no way he was getting his first butt off of me.

I pulled his backpack up on his shoulders again when we got to Eddie's front door.

"Tell Eddie's mom I'll pick you up at four-thirty."

"Pip?"

I could feel that joint in my sock. I would have lit it right there if I could.

"What?"

"Who puts the *m*'s on the M&M's?"

I should have seen something like that coming.

"An elf," I told him. "A purple one with lots of paintbrushes."

"Really?"

"No."

Mikey looked at me like I had something growing out of my forehead.

"What are you gawking at? Go on. Eddie's waiting for you at the door."

He kept standing there, so I took off. I flipped my cigarette butt into the street, then looked back to see if he'd gone in yet. He was still watching me.

Man. Sometimes he looks so young—so little.

"What?" I asked him, and put my hands up over my head.

He waved to me and I nodded back real quick before breaking into a sprint. I pulled another cigarette out of my pack and lit it on my way to the only place I can ever go where nobody hassles me.

I want to hold my breath for as long as it takes.

I want to stop breathing just long enough to know what it would be like to be totally still.

Like being just a cough away from death.

Not really there—not really here.

I got a lot of friends. Some of them are dead. Some of them are on their way. All of them hang out at what I call the Site. It's this one part of the Mountain of Hope Cemetery where there's a whole slew of real old graves nobody visits anymore. I bet anybody who knew these people is six feet under now too.

One of my friends at the Site is George Beattie, Beloved Husband, Loving Father, born 1875, died 1925. He knows me as good as anybody. There's Agnes, who I'm pretty tight with too. Agnes Jaffe, Devoted Wife and Friend. She's right next to George.

After I dropped Mikey off at Eddie's, I went to the Site. I knew my guys were going to be there. We're always there. It's where we hang out and nobody can find us—not that anybody is looking. It's also where Johnny passes out the stash, and I was pretty low on supply that day. The joint in my sock was all I had left.

"Pip, man," Slayer yells to me from in front of Robert Hahn, 1817–1878. "Where the hell you been?"

Frankie got the name Slayer after he dyed his buzz cut and his eyebrows white. His skin is almost gray and he's got the reddest freakin' lips you ever saw on a guy that wasn't wearing a dress. He looks just like the skinny guy on that *Buffy the Vampire Slayer* show. None of us knew his name so we just started calling him the Slayer guy. Frankie thought it was so cool, he got *Slayer* tattooed on his arm, right over his wrist, with a dagger going through the *y*.

"I went over to the Dumpster looking for you after sixth period," he said. "Friggin' Tony came out and grubbed my last roach." Slayer took a drink from a bottle he was holding, then passed it up to me.

I grabbed it.

"Got snagged by Giraldi today," I told him. "I had to hit all my classes."

"No way." Johnny stood up in front of George Beattie and we knocked shoulders.

"I'm in deep, man," I told them, then took a drink from the bottle. I didn't even care what I was drinking. I had an edge on me so sharp, I could slice something just by looking at it. It was going to take a hell of a lot of drink and smoke to keep from cutting myself on me.

"Giraldi's after my ass."

"What's his problem?" Johnny dropped back down on his butt and leaned against George. I sat in front of Agnes.

"If I don't go to every class, he's kickin' my ass out of school and calling the old man to tell him about it."

"Then we'd have to dig you a nice hole in the ground right here next to George and Agnes," Johnny said, and Slayer started laughing.

"No joke," I said, thinking about how I almost wet my pants when Giraldi had my father's office on the line.

Johnny lit up a joint and held it out to me. "So just go to classes for a couple of weeks. Then he'll forget you just like everybody else does."

"I don't think so," I said, hoping my head would stop racing. "Not this time."

I didn't tell the guys about Giraldi blackmailing me—nothing about the counseling. If those guys thought I was going to talk to anybody, they'd start looking over their shoulders. They wouldn't trust me anymore.

They weren't going to know about the counseling—if I went.

"Don't let Giraldi get to your old man," Johnny said. "Just do what you got to do to keep that phone from ringing."

Johnny knew what he was talking about. He'd seen my father in action a couple of times. You don't forget that. Back when me and Johnny were in the seventh grade, right after his father split, he came over a lot. He saw things. He heard. He knows.

I don't go to Johnny's apartment too much anymore either. Somewhere around the eighth grade his place started smelling funky. Everything was always a mess, old pizza on the table, dishes and cruddy pots in the sink. His mother is a garbage-head who keeps herself in supply by trading her body for drugs.

I'm the only one of us guys who knows about that. Me and

Johnny go back to junior high. We go back to when we didn't know enough to keep our mouths shut and our front doors off-limits.

"What are you going to do?" Slayer handed me back the bottle and I took another long pull on it before answering him.

"After I drop my brother off at school in the mornings, I'm gonna get myself behind the Dumpster and smoke as much weed as I can before first period. I'm going to try and grab a few hits out the bathroom window between classes."

Slayer shook his head. "You're going to have to, man. You'll never make it all day without a buzz. I keep a bottle in my locker and get a bathroom pass so I can take a few swigs when the hall is empty."

"See you tomorrow fourth period?" I asked him.

"I'm there." Slayer put his fist out and I hit mine on top of it. Then he put his Walkman headphones on and leaned back against Robert Hahn's cement pillow. He had the damn music cranked so loud, I could hear the exact song he was blasting.

The pictures in my head were slowing down. I didn't see Fleming anymore, with her finger slamming into my brain. Giraldi's hand on the phone was a blur. I couldn't see Jenna watching me walk out of class . . . Coach Fredericks blowing his whistle . . . Mikey waving good-bye.

"Pip," Johnny said, sounding like he had cotton in his mouth. "I figured out a way you can get some driving lessons."

"Hm?" I had my eyes closed. I took a couple of quick inhales on the joint.

"We can get some cash together real easy for you if you want. One of those dorky driving schools, you know, with the signs on the roof, could take you on the road."

"How?"

"Mo is setting me up."

"With a driving school?" I still had my eyes closed. I didn't really want to talk.

"I'm going to sell for him."

Mo is this guy in the Bronx who Johnny takes the train to see once or twice a week to pick up stash. I went with him a couple of times. Slayer takes the ride once in a while. But Johnny goes every week. He gets enough product to sell to the two of us, but I never heard of him dealing to anybody else.

"I'm going to get me some serious money, Pip. I'm going to unload so much weed and coke and ecstasy for this guy, I'm going to be rich. You can get in on this with me if you want."

I opened my eyes and looked over at Johnny. He was staring at me like he really wanted me to go in on it with him.

"I don't know," I said. We never say no to each other, me and Johnny. If he wants to sneak into a movie, we go. If I want to kick somebody's ass for giving me trouble, he's right there. We don't say no. We say I don't know.

"What do you mean, you don't know. Forget money for driving lessons. You could get enough cash to buy your own wheels. Hell, if Giraldi kicks you out, we'll buy you your own *school*."

"I'm so wasted right now, Johnny. I can't think about nothin'."

"I hear you." He leaned back against the headstone.

"I could use another bag now, though," I told him.

Johnny shook his head and shoved a small bag of pot at my chest.

"Here," he said. "But I'm not covering you forever. You're going to have to get a job. Go price peas at the damn Stop and

Shop if you're not going in on this with me, but I'm not covering you forever."

"I'll get you money for the bag."

"How about for the last three I spotted you?"

"It's coming," I told him. But I didn't have any paper money at all. I had a few quarters and a dime.

"We could be a couple of very rich assholes," Johnny said.

I took a last hit off the joint and flicked the rest away before it burned my thumb.

"Anyway," he said, "come out with us tonight. We're crashing some cheerleader's party. I'm bringing the bong and a case of Bud."

"What time?"

Just when he said eight o'clock, I jumped up.

"What time is it?"

Johnny clicked his lighter in front of a cigarette. "Ten after five," he said.

"Crap," I yelled, then ran my ass through the cemetery, jumping over a couple of freshly covered holes in the ground.

It was after five.

I forgot to pick up Mikey.

I remember when my mother came home from the hospital with the baby. He was getting all kinds of presents he couldn't even use yet—stuffed bears, trucks, blocks.

I didn't get anything.

Mom looked like crap. She needed something but I didn't know what.

I guess Dad didn't either, because we left.

It started out as a long drive. He didn't say anything. Then we ended

up at some stupid G-rated movie. I mean, I was ten. I could have han-
dled something with a little more punch to it.
But it was better than staying home smelling diapers and listening
to the baby cry—watching Mom cry.
So we had popcorn, ate Goobers, and watched the movie.
Twice.

I crunched down on a Pepomint LifeSaver as I walked into
my house. My clothes reeked as if they'd been on fire, and my
shoes smelled like rum. Maybe I'd spilled some. Anybody else
would have changed his clothes—maybe showered.

Not me. I'd go only as far as a LifeSaver. It didn't matter anyway. Nobody living in my house knows how to connect the
dots. They don't have a clue about me.

I always figured I was like the family dog—like a puppy
people get when it's all cute and fuzzy. Then when it's full-
grown, they send the mutt to live out back on the end of some
chain. He doesn't look for anybody to play with, or to brush
him or pat his head. He learns not to want. He learns that
being outside's a better way to deal than being inside anyway.
He thinks about getting the leash off—finding his own Ken-L
Ration.

My house was quiet when I walked in. It's always either quieter than the Site or louder than Yankee Stadium when the
score is tied in the ninth.

Everybody was sitting at the kitchen table eating dinner. My
mother shot me a look. It was either for being late or because
my father just finished screaming about me being late.

"Wash your hands," she said.

Yeah, I had a great day. Thanks for asking.

I went over to the sink, squirted some soap into my hands, and squished them together under the tap.

Nobody was talking. Mikey didn't even look up at me. He was pissed. Boo-hoo, I forgot to pick him up. The kid better grow up fast. He was still breathing. He got home fine.

My father—a.k.a. the Grinch, because he can steal Christmas from you way before December 25 comes around—had both his elbows on the table. He was jabbing at his food with his fork as if the chicken wasn't dead yet. He was in his shoot-to-kill mood. I could tell just by looking at him.

His face gets red, his ears go back a little, and his eyes stick out of his face like Mr. Potato Head. He doesn't smile when he's being the Grinch. No. The Grinch never smiles in that old cartoon either. He does the same thing my father does—he smirks. It's like he's telling you that you're the biggest idiot in the world, but he's doing it without making a sound.

As soon as I sat down, the family fun time got rolling. The Grinch pushed his plate into my mother's, sending a couple of macaroni and cheese noodles onto the side of her water glass.

"You call this a meal?" he asked. The noodles started sliding down from the glass to the table.

"There's nothing wrong with that chicken," she said in a voice that was just asking for a fight. Sometimes I think she *wants* him to scream and throw things at her. Just by looking at my father's face, anybody—except maybe my stupid brother—could see the guy's nuts. If my mother said something like, *I'll fix you something else* and just let it go at that, maybe the rest of us could finish our food for a change.

He reached across the table with his fork and stabbed another piece of chicken. After he put it in his mouth he scrunched up his face like a little kid would. He spit it back onto his plate and started yelling.

"That's disgusting! I don't work all day to come home and eat bland rubber."

I put the saltshaker in front of him.

"Are you a wiseass?" he asked me.

First Giraldi called me a wiseass, then my father. I was a trendsetter.

"Maybe it just needs some salt," I said, but didn't really care if he liked his friggin' chicken or not. I just wanted him to get off her back. The best way to do that was to get him yelling at me instead.

Mikey wasn't chewing but had a mouthful of food. I could tell he was trying not to cry.

This family fighting stuff rattles him a lot more than it ever did me when I was six. Sometimes I wish I could press the Pause button on our family like on a VCR. Our family isn't any G-rated flick, so I'd just get the kid out of the audience. I'd drop him off someplace else, come back by myself, then press Play.

"I'll reheat you a leftover," my mother said. She went over to the counter, and my father got up and rinsed out his glass.

I heard ice cubes rattling behind me. The Grinch was busy doing what he does best: fixing himself a drink. He keeps the bottles lined up like soldiers at attention on top of the refrigerator, and pulls them down for active duty. I heard the ice cubes crack when the scotch hit them, same as always. Then Mike Senior shook the glass to mix it up, making the cubes clang against the sides.

Some families listen to music while they eat, mine listens to ice cubes.

He put the bottle back on top of the fridge—back in the line-up—and sat down again.

"You look like hell," he said to me.

"I'm tired," I said.

"Tired? Must be all that studying you do."

"Mike, don't start," my mother said, coming back to the table with a plate of steaming beef teriyaki.

"Oh, okay, Eve. Why don't you warm the baby's bottle for him." He took a long drink from his glass. His eyes were getting redder and redder.

He looked back at me. "You ever clean out the garage like I've been asking you?"

"I started it—"

"Get out there and finish."

"Mike, he's eating," my mother said, forgetting I could take care of myself.

"I'll eat later, Mom."

"You're not eating until that garage is clean."

I gave Mikey's shoulder a squeeze when I walked behind him. He still had the same mouthful of food.

"Swallow," I whispered to him, but I don't think he heard me. My parents were screaming at each other. Dad was telling Mom she babies us, and she was calling him a bully. Same old stuff.

The phone rang just when I was walking by it, so I took the call.

"Hello?"

"Is this Phillip?" the voice on the other end asked.

"It's Pip," I said.

"This is Mr. Giraldi."

I thought I was going to hurl right there on the kitchen floor.

I didn't say a word. I put my hand over the mouthpiece so he wouldn't hear all the screaming behind me, and pulled the cord as far as I could into the living room.

"I was calling to speak to your father," he said.

"I thought we had a deal."

"I called Ms. Butler today. She said you never called her. That was *your* end of the deal."

My father was yelling pretty loud. There was no way Giraldi couldn't hear it, no matter how tight I had my hand on the mouthpiece.

"I am not playing around," he said. "You can't stop me every time I try to call."

"I'll call her now."

"She's not in." He was quiet for a second. Maybe he was listening to my father call my mother names I'd get detention for using in class. "You'd better call her first thing in the morning and have an appointment for the afternoon. If you don't, while you're off smoking dope or doing whatever it is you do, I'll be on the phone with your father."

"I hear you."

"Get the hell off the phone," my father yelled.

"Do the right thing, Phillip," Giraldi said. "This is your last chance. See it for what it is."

Then I heard a dial tone.

I want a vote in my own life.

I hung up, thinking anybody looking at me could see my heart beating under my shirt.

I started walking past my father to the door, but he stopped his yelling right in the middle of a sentence to grab my elbow. He leaned in and sniffed my shoulder.

"What's that smell? You smell like—what the hell is that?"

I wondered if my parents ever smoked pot. If he figured out the smell, I wasn't going to be cleaning the garage. I was going to be picking out my casket.

"Wood shop," I told him. "It stinks up my clothes."

"Do you ever wash, for cryin' out loud?"

"You want me to clean the garage or take a shower?"

"I want you to get the hell out of here before I puke."

Like he never does that.

I was thinking, What does he care how I smell? He just wants to put me down. The guy has a whole list on me. I'm stupid, I don't listen, I'm a smart-ass, a slob, and now I stink too.

Screw him. He doesn't know anything about me.

Asshole.

I don't take wood shop.

It's like I'm trapped inside somebody else's life.
Somebody else's family.
I want out.

Even from inside the garage I could hear my parents yelling at each other.

How could I be related to these people? Maybe someday the truth would come out that I was really left at their door by gypsies. Maybe that was why my brother was named Junior and not me.

I don't look like any of them. Mikey has our father's dark curly hair and blue eyes. Mom and I have brown eyes, but hers are round like pizzas and mine are like footballs. I'm the only Downs with blond hair, and nobody on my mom's side of the family is blond either.

I had no idea where to start in the garage. My father had been yelling at me for weeks to clean it. I kept saying yeah, yeah, but this was the first time I'd seen the inside of the place in months.

I looked around. None of the crap in there was mine, but for some stupid reason I was the one who had to clean it. There was an old box fan with a spider family hanging out in between the slats, an air conditioner, eight million extension cords, and an old dresser. There were about eight half-empty bottles of detergent and twenty other cans and bottles of cleaners probably from back when George Beattie was alive. There were Christmas decorations, rusted tools, and jelly jars filled with nails and screws. There were boxes and boxes of crap, a ton of dirt, and way too many bugs.

"Whoooooosh!" My brother came running in with his red Superman cape flying from the back of his neck. He made a swooshing sound all around the garage, trying to be faster than a speeding bullet. Then he made believe he was landing right in front of me.

"Metropolis is safe," he said. "I got the bad guys."

"You beat up Dad?"

He didn't answer me. It's a trick he uses that he learned from his big brother.

I pushed a few boxes around. One of them felt more solid, better packed, than the others. I pulled open the flaps and looked inside. All I could see was rolled-up newspaper. I unwrapped one roll and inside was a statue of a boy with a big head and a very white face.

"Look at this, Bugs. Mom used to collect these. She packed them away when you were two years old because you couldn't keep your paws off anything."

"Why not?"

"Why not what? Why couldn't you keep your paws off anything? Because you were two years old and a pain in the butt—kind of like you are now."

I re-wrapped the statue and put it back in the box. I wondered if Mom had forgotten she had them.

"Pip?"

"What?"

"Why do they call them M&M's? Why don't they call them G&G's or B&B's?"

"Who cares?"

"Me."

"Don't you care about anything else?"

"Yes. I just wanted to know."

"So go on www.whogivesacrapaboutm&m's.com."

I pushed some paint cans to the side, and Mikey started zooming around the garage again. Then he just stopped. "Pip?"

"What now, Bugs?"

"Do you love Daddy?"

I should have let him stick to the candy questions.

"Do *you*?" I asked him.

"I think so."

I opened another box and found a bunch of rotted old Tinkertoys that smelled like garbage.

"Pip?"

"What?"

"Does Daddy love me?"

I wasn't sure if I felt sorry for the kid or if I felt like slugging him. All I wanted to do was grab a couple of hits off a joint and have a beer with the guys.

But I was stuck in the garage with Super-Stupid-Question-Man.

"What do you think, Bugs?"

"Yes?"

"Listen, I got a lot to do in here. Could you cut me a break and scram?"

He stuck his tongue out at me and went back to zooming around the garage. He had his arms out like airplane wings. Three seconds later, faster than a speeding idiot, a stack of boxes went crashing to the floor and stuff spilled out all over the place.

"Oops," he said, friggin' genius that he is.

"Nice job, butthead. Now put it all back."

He bent down to pick stuff up. Then he came over to me with a handful of bottle caps.

"What's all this?" he asked.

I couldn't believe it. I thought I'd thrown them out a hundred years ago.

"That's my old bottle cap collection."

I used to collect every kind of bottle cap I could find—back when I was young enough to think stupid stuff like that mattered.

"Can I have them?" Bugs asked.

Why not? I wasn't using them.

"If you pick up everything you knocked over, you can take the bottle caps. But you have to get lost—take them out of here."

I looked at some before tossing them back into their box. I remembered every cap. I knew where I'd gotten each one and how hard some of them were to find. Dr Pepper, grape Nehi, Yoo-Hoo, Chocolate Cow—they were all there.

Mikey took off flying with the box under his arm. I leaned my back against the wall and looked down at my closed fist. I opened my hand and stared at the cap I was holding—the one I didn't put back in the box. The one I'd decided I didn't want Mikey to have.

It was a Budweiser cap. It was from off the top of my first beer.

The one my father gave me.

I was nine.

I want to collect something.
Not comic books or baseball cards.
It has to be something real.
Maybe dust.

It got dark out and I figured Mom was putting Mikey to bed. By eight o'clock I knew the Grinch was sitting in front of the TV with a glass in his hand. There was no way he was thinking about how far I was getting in the garage. He'd been telling me for weeks to clean it and then kept forgetting to check if I ever did. That night wasn't going to be any different. I knew they'd forgotten about me in the garage. You know, the whole family dog thing.

So I left the garage pretty much the way I found it. I moved some boxes from here to there. Swept some crap into a pile.

Then I walked the mile to that party Johnny had talked about crashing.

He was there, passing a pipe around so nobody would ask him to leave. We get to crash parties without too much trouble as long as he supplies some of the party favors. Nobody asked us to go.

Not until Slayer pulled the knife.

I didn't see what happened. I was out back under the cheerleader's deck, smoking a bone and finishing off my fourth Bud.

I was watching Jenna across the yard. It was dark and I was wasted, but I could see her. I couldn't miss her. She has this way of moving that isn't like any other girl I know. She moves her shoulders when she talks and tips her head to one side a lot.

Right before all the noise started, she walked by.

"Hey," I said.

She turned to look at me and smiled.

It was *that* smile.

"How's it going?" I asked.

She took a couple of steps my way. "I'm not much of a party person," she said.

"Maybe this will help." I held my joint out for her to take.

"Is it helping *you*?" she asked, not making a move to take it out of my hand.

I took a hit off the joint and held my breath, keeping my eyes on her.

"You're out here alone," she said. "You're under a porch, and you don't look like you're having any fun."

I blew the smoke out behind me. "I'm not alone." I smiled. "I'm with you."

"I was just heading inside to get a soda."

"I'll come with you." I put the the joint out on the bottom of my shoe and shoved the rest of it into my sock. Grabbing my half-empty bottle of beer, I stood next to her. But she didn't move.

"Ever go a day without that stuff?" she asked me.

"What do you think I am? A total waste?"

"What do *you* think you are, Pip?"

"Just me," I said, feeling high from standing next to her.

Jenna started walking, and we made our way up the deck steps. I could hear the yelling from outside the door. When I pulled it open, I knew something was up. Guys were cursing, girls were screeching. I took off from Jenna and ran into the living room to make sure my boys were okay. Slayer had his pocketknife out and was facing off with one of the football players.

"I told you to step away from my girl," the guy was yelling with his finger pointing at Slayer.

"She was on my lap." Slayer flicked some blood off his lip. "She's very friendly."

The jock took a swing, and Slayer swiped at him with the knife and missed. This wasn't going to be good.

I shot Johnny a look. He was thinking what I was thinking. I put up one finger at a time, counting to three. On three Johnny and I jumped the jock. Johnny got him from behind in a headlock, I twisted his arm back, and Slayer came our way. I let go of the jock, grabbed the knife out of Slayer's hand, and took off out the front door. Johnny held the jock while Slayer nailed him a few shots to the gut.

I ran a block down the street and dropped the knife down the sewer. The cops were going to show up for this fight—that much I knew. A knife on anybody was going to mean a trip to the precinct. That was worse than getting kicked out of school. I was covering my own ass as much as Slayer's.

When I ran back into the living room, fists were flying and stuff was breaking. I took a few hits to the face and knocked somebody into a cabinet that had a hell of a lot of plates in it.

"Cops!" somebody yelled, and half the guys that were fighting took off. I had a fullback pushing me into a corner, throwing punches into my kidneys so I couldn't get out of there.

As I watched four cops run in, I noticed Jenna looking at me. She wasn't smiling.

I looked away and took a sharp hit to the chest.

I remember the first time I had a bad trip.

Johnny had got our stash from somebody besides Mo. He said it was superior, top grade.

We smoked a lot of it. It was laced with something, but we didn't know what.

I saw things flying around the cemetery—things scarier than ghosts. My head felt as if somebody was squeezing it. My heart was racing. I thought people were hiding behind trees staring at me. I was afraid that any second there was going to be a nuclear attack and we were all going to die.

Johnny thought it was the best high he'd ever had.

"Let's get some more of that," he said.

I remember wishing I had some way to stop—to stop going places I didn't want to go. Places with too many surprises. Places I didn't know my way around.

"You seem like a smart kid," Officer Wanna-Be-Your-Pal was saying.

He was driving the squad car with me in the front seat, my

head leaning on the window. I felt like I was going to puke. He kept talking like this was the Big Brother program or something. How there's more to life than drugs and fighting. This road is only going to lead me into tunnels I can't get out of. Crazy stuff like that. I didn't hear half of what he was saying. I did a lot of shoulder shrugging—a bunch of I dunno's.

The whole thing sucked. The jocks only got a good talkin' to, but Johnny, Slayer, and I all got rides home in cop cars. I think it was because we're the ones with the long hair, tattoos, and earrings. Cops hate guys like us.

Getting brought home by a cop is pretty bad, but I wasn't flipping out like I did in Giraldi's office. I'd done so much partying that I wasn't feeling any pain and I couldn't really give a crap. Besides, getting in trouble for fighting wasn't going to get me thrown out of the house or tossed into rehab like being expelled would.

And I figured that if my old man was still awake, he'd be more tanked up than me and I could outrun him.

"This is it?" Officer Pal asked, pulling into the driveway.

"Home sweet home," I said.

"What's going to happen when your parents open the door?"

"Keep your hand on your revolver," I told him.

"The way you crack jokes, it's like you don't really care. It's like nothing rattles you."

One of the upsides to getting high.

We got out of the cruiser and walked halfway up the driveway. Then I stopped, bent over, and hurled.

One of the downsides to partying.

The cop waited for me. He stepped back so I wouldn't splash his shoes.

"You all right?" he asked when I started to stand up again.

"I never ate dinner tonight," I told him, wiping my mouth on my shoulder.

"If you're going to drink, you should eat."

What he didn't know was that trying to eat in my house could make you just as sick.

"You know what?" I asked, looking around like I was confused. "This isn't my house. I live down the block."

He kept walking, then rang the doorbell. As soon as it started to open, I was back on my knees, puking up some stringy green crap.

I couldn't hear what anybody was saying. I couldn't even hear if it was my mother's voice or my father's. The cop was only there for about a minute. He walked past me, stepping over my spew.

"Try to stay off my shift," he said. "The next time you're in trouble on my clock, I'm bringing you in. Got it?"

He dropped a business card next to my knee on the ground. "There's my number at the precinct. If I can help keep that trouble from happening, call me."

Everybody wanted to help me. I could play poker with all the business cards I was getting.

His car door slammed shut, the engine started, and he drove off.

I didn't look over at the front door. I didn't move. If it was my father standing there, I had to get ready to run. If it was my mother, I wasn't so sure I wanted to see her face—or have her see mine.

"Pip." It was my mother.

I was still on my knees looking at the ground. My mother's slippers stopped right in front of me.

I tipped my head to look up. The sky did a little flip and I saw her face. She looked like I felt—all washed out from a shit day. She looked tired, sad maybe, even ready to throw up.

I think I make her sick sometimes.

"Come into the house." She put a hand out and helped me stand. "Wash your face, brush your teeth, and get into bed. Try to do it without waking your father. I don't want to be up listening to him all night."

She went inside. I watched the back of her head walking away from me.

I dragged myself into the house and up the stairs to my room, stopping to throw up in the bathroom on the way. I kicked my shoes off in the hall, went into my room, and jabbed my foot stepping on an action figure. I told that kid to stop playing in my room.

I stood next to the bed, pulled off my jeans, and some quarters fell out on the floor. I took off my socks and then grabbed everything I had just put on the floor and shoved it all under the mattress.

I flopped onto the bed and hit my head on something hard.

It moved.

It was my brother.

"Pip," he said. "What are you doing in my bed? Did you have a bad dream?"

I closed my eyes.

I was so wasted and tired, I couldn't even tell him to shut up.

I want to know what it's like to wake up in the morning and be glad I did.

■ ■ ■

I opened my eyes. Everything was fuzzy. I felt as if someone was slamming his foot into my head over and over again. Mikey was sitting cross-legged next to me on the mattress.

"How come you went to sleep in my bed?" he asked.

"You're in *my* bed, skank-ball." My mouth felt like a mix of sand and Elmer's glue.

He chomped into a cookie, and eight million crumbs fell on my face. "Look," he said. "These are my Superman sheets."

He was right. I sat up to look around. The Superman posters, stuffed animals, Legos, and action figures started spinning.

"Oh crap." I put my hand over my mouth and ran into the bathroom. There wasn't really anything left for me to throw up. I kept spitting and spitting, and my mouth tasted like dried-up Play-Doh.

Mikey pushed the door open into my foot. "Daddy's in the bathroom downstairs," he said. "He's doing the same thing as you."

I saw his arm come at me, and I tried to swat it away. He pulled something off the back of my head and smiled.

"I was looking for that," he said, and showed me the half an Oreo he'd taken off of my head. If he put it in his mouth I was going to hurl again.

"Turn the shower on for me, Bugs."

He put his two hands together over his head and tossed the cookie into the garbage pail next to me like he was taking a foul shot.

He turned the shower on. "Pip?"

I stood up as much as I could without falling over. "What?"

"Are you and Daddy sick?"

Another one of my brother's genius questions.

"Get me some clothes," I said.

"Daddy throws up a lot."

"I don't feel like talking to you right now, Bugs. Get me my damn clothes."

He walked out, and I dragged myself under the water nozzle. I needed to get my sorry ass in gear. If I missed first period Giraldi was going to have me hung and shot.

After I finished soaking my head I leaned out of the shower to yell to Mikey to bring me my stupid clothes. I was just about to call him when I saw that on the floor right next to the toilet was a blue tie-dyed T-shirt, a pair of Levi's, and my purple boxers.

I got dressed and went into my room to find my stash. I wasn't going to be able to make it to all my classes if I didn't get a little weed in me before school. I looked on my dresser, on the floor, next to my pillow, in the bathroom, inside my shoes.

Then I remembered.

I walked into Mikey's room to check under the mattress, but I didn't have to. He was sitting on the floor with my bag of weed in his hand. He licked his finger, stuck it in the bag, and ate what he pulled out.

"What the hell are you doing?" I grabbed the bag out of his hand.

"Having a snack," he said.

"You're an idiot," I growled, and shoved it into my front pocket.

"It's mine," he whined. "It was sticking out of my bed."

I lifted the mattress and grabbed the other things I'd stuffed there the night before.

"Get out of my room," he yelled at me, looking like he was going to start crying.

"Don't touch my stuff." I was getting loud.

"It's my room," he shouted.

"It's going to be your *ass* in a minute if you don't shut up."

My mother walked in like she was ready to put out a fire. "What's going on in here?"

"Pip's being a jerk." Mikey was still whining, and I was holding back from whacking him one.

"Go downstairs and have your breakfast," she told the baby.

"I want a new brother," he yelled, walking out.

"You can have one," I yelled back. "Get some other chump to walk your nose-picking face to school every morning—"

"Don't treat your brother like that," she said. "He looks up to you."

"Tell him to stop."

She was pissed. "Someday he will," she said, grabbing my elbow for a sec, then dropping it. "Someday he *won't* look up to you, and you'll miss it."

"He's a creepy pain in the butt, Mom. I'm tired of him tagging along all the time. Can't Eddie Farrot's mother drive him home after school?"

"No. You can do it."

"I'm not his father," I said.

"You're his brother."

"So what? That means I've got to walk him to school, pick him up, and watch him every day?"

"Yes."

I was about to let loose on her that it's really her job to take care of him, not mine. But she kept talking.

"When I saw that policeman at our front door last night," she said, "I thought he was going to tell me you were dead."

She was getting ready to cry. I could tell. I knew that look. It was the same one she gets when my father yells at her.

"Your father wants to be the way he is, that's his choice. You're the way *you* are and I'm too late to save you." She looked as if she was in pain—as if I had taken a knife and jammed it into her gut.

"But your brother," she said. "He still has a chance. Things could be different for him."

She put her hand under my chin. "I can't have all three of you out of control. I can't live like this—the screaming, the throwing things, the middle of the night fights, and now the police bringing you home. I can't take any more and I won't allow your brother to get himself messed up too."

She dropped her hand from my chin and used it to wipe the tears off her face.

"Mikey's coach called," she said. "He's been missing T-ball practice. Take him there after school today."

I didn't answer.

"You hear me?"

"I hear you," I said.

"Don't make your brother late for school," she said, and left me standing there staring at the door—watching the back of her head walk away again.

I guess it was better than seeing that look on her face—those sad brown eyes that don't look even a little like mine.

I remember one day when I was eight years old. It was snowing. I wanted to go out and play. But I couldn't ask my parents because they were busy yelling at each other.

My father threw something at the wall, then I saw him grab my mother by the arm and push her out the front door. I ran to the window and saw her standing on the porch with her arms across her chest.

She had no coat, no boots, just a pair of pink fuzzy slippers that were getting wet fast.

The kids across the street were making snow angels on their lawn.

I knew Bugs couldn't keep quiet all the way to school. I figured halfway there he'd forget he was mad and hit me with a bunch of stupid questions. He held out 'til we got right in front of Ann Hutch Elementary.

"Who's stronger?" he asked. "Spider-Man, Batman, or Superman?"

I told him what he wanted to hear. "Superman can kick anybody's butt."

"Who's stronger? You or Daddy?"

"What do you think?"

"You?" He didn't sound too sure.

"I got kryptonite in my pocket," I said, hitting the front of my jeans. "Superman can't even get near me."

"Check it out," he yelled, pointing to the backhoe digging away at that hole in front of the school. "Maybe they're building a swimming pool."

"Not in the front of the school, bean head."

"I'm going to be a construction worker when I grow up," he said. "I'm going to dig holes and fix things."

"You better get into school or we're both going to be late."

"Know what?" He pulled his backpack up on his shoulders. "Daddy's going on a class trip with me."

All I could do was blink. Once.

"We're going to the zoo," he said.

Don't hold your breath, I almost answered.

"He's going to be a leprechaun," Mikey said.

"You mean a chaperone."

"Uh-huh."

"You know, Bugs, sometimes Dad says he's going to do something, then he doesn't."

"Like taking us to the beach—"

"Right."

"And to McDonald's that time—"

"Yeah and—"

"But not this time."

"How do you know, Mikey?"

"He promised."

I blinked again. "Oh," I said.

He turned to the school, but stopped for one more question.

"Pip, what was that stuff this morning? That stuff you got so mad at me for eating?"

I made like I didn't hear him and walked away.

Maybe he'd forget to ask me later—if I was lucky.

Maybe he'd stick to asking about M&M's.

TWO

I want to be a rock star.

I want to bang on the drums or wail a guitar so loud, it blows my ears out.

Then I wouldn't have to hear anything.

School sucked. All day.

It started with Giraldi grabbing me on my way to first period.

"Did you make your call?"

Crap. I knew I'd screwed something up.

I checked my pockets to see if I still had the counselor's business card while Giraldi sort of shoved me into his office. If I hadn't had it on me, I think Giraldi would have called my father right there on the spot.

I held it up. "See? I was going to call. I was just on my way to a pay phone."

I started to leave and he blocked my way.

"Call now," he said.

"It's kind of private. You know what I mean?"

"If you don't use the phone on my desk right now, I'll be making my own call."

I picked up the receiver and started to dial the number on the card. I felt funny being on his side of the desk while he was where I'm always standing. I thought about giving him a detention.

I sat down on his chair and leaned back to get comfortable. I sort of sank into the chair and started swiveling back and forth.

"You've got to be kidding!" He came at me and put his finger on the phone like I'd done the day before.

"Stand up," he said, pulling on my elbow.

I stood.

"You don't seem to understand, Phillip—"

"Pip—"

"Quiet. I'm giving you a chance to turn your life around. I'm paying attention to something going on with you that no one else has bothered to do anything about. I am giving you a shot here."

"Yeah, some shot. More like blackmail."

"That's the way you see it?"

"I see you threatening me."

"What you don't see, Mr. Downs, is that I'm the best friend you ever had."

He nodded his head toward the phone and stepped away so I could dial.

"Jensen Family Counseling," a woman's voice said on the other end.

"Can I talk to Claire Butler?"

"This is Claire."

I was hoping she wasn't going to be in. I mean, I knew I had to do this or get killed—I just didn't want to do it right that second.

"My principal told me to call so I can come in and see you."

"What's your name?"

"Pip Downs."

"Oh, right. Mr. Giraldi told me you'd be calling—yesterday."

"Well, I'm calling today."

"I'm glad you did. Mr. Giraldi said that he thought you could use someone to talk to—that you have a lot going on right now."

"He wouldn't know," I said.

"He also told me that he wants you to sign a release form giving me permission to let him know whether or not you show for appointments and comply with the counseling. Are you okay with that?"

"Did he tell you I don't have a choice?"

I looked at Giraldi. He had his hands in his pockets and was watching me.

"He said if you didn't come in he was expelling you."

"Nice guy, right?"

"Can you make it in today right after school? Say, three-thirty?"

"I have to take my brother to T-ball practice—"

"I don't want to hear excuses," Giraldi jumped in. "You get yourself there."

"What time is his practice?" Claire asked.

"Three-thirty 'til about four-thirty."

"Can you get to my office by five?"

"Probably."

She told me where the office was. It wasn't far from the school. I knew the place. It was right next to the all-night gas station mini-mart where the Friday cashier always lets us buy six-packs.

I hung up the phone and Giraldi opened his office door for me to step out.

"You have to attend all of the counseling appointments as often as she says and follow her rules. If you cut counseling or classes you're out of here."

"Wouldn't you have more fun hassling somebody else?" I asked as I walked out the door.

"No," he said.

"Best friend I ever had, my ass," I said loud enough for him to hear.

I want to go to a new kind of school.

A school that teaches you what you need to know—not what you're supposed to know.

The third-floor boys' bathroom smelled like a mix of everything that's ever been flushed down the toilet plus the B.O. of a hundred ballplayers. I did my part to get rid of the stench by lighting up a joint next to an open window. There was no way I was going to sit through Fleming's class without a little help from my friend Mr. Cannabis the Weed.

I sucked in as much freedom as I could, holding on to the smoke until my lungs were going to bust.

"Can I get a hit?" this kid Webster asked me, coming out of one of the stalls. Johnny and I gave him the name Webster because he's like a friggin' walking dictionary. This is the kind of guy who's always trying to get somebody like me to like him. Trying to come off cool by asking for a *hit* or laughing too loud when you're acting stupid. I don't know why these bozos can't just be okay with who they are—smart losers who'll never be cool but will make a lot of money someday.

"No time, Webster. I can't be late for class."

I breathed in some more life and closed my eyes, hoping the kid would disappear. He didn't.

"You're *always* late for class," he said, laughing at his joke. I didn't laugh with him. I didn't even smile. I blew some smoke his way and stared him down until he left.

I pulled as much from the roach as I could—smoking it down so low that I burned my lip.

I was splashing water on my mouth to cool it when the late bell rang and the bathroom door opened. I figured it was going to be Giraldi or some hall monitor to bust me.

It was Slayer.

He was getting ready to light up a bone.

"Here," he said. "I got one for you too."

I was late already. A few more minutes wouldn't kill anybody.

I want to know what teachers talk about in the teachers' lounge.
I bet the guy teachers hit each other in the arm, talking about the

tenth-grade girls in their tight jeans. They probably go on about how they wish those same girls had been in their high school back when they were pimply-faced teenagers.

I want to know who the teachers are when they aren't teaching.

I had my excuse all ready.

I was going to tell Fleming that I helped Josie the cafeteria lady pick up a bunch of chocolate milk cartons she'd dropped outside the kitchen. Josie hurt her right elbow and needed me to carry the milk for her. I put my notebook down to help her, but when I went back to get it, it was gone. I went into all the classes near the kitchen to see if anybody had found it, and some kid Jerry said he had brought it to the main office. By the time I got it back, the bell had already rung and I was late for her class.

It was the perfect lie—full of solid details.

But merry freakin' Christmas! Fleming wasn't there. We had a sub.

"Sorry I'm late," I said, ready to go into my milk carton story.

"That's okay. Glad you could make it. I'm Mr. Kirkland." The sub smiled at me as if we were old friends. I'd never seen the guy before in my life. "Take a seat wherever you like," he said.

There was a free spot right next to Jenna. She sits in the first row and normally I'd never be caught dead up front, but I headed right for it anyway. I didn't know how she was going to feel about it. She's not the kind of girl who hangs out with guys on their way to having a rap sheet, and the last time she'd seen me I had a cop for a chauffeur.

"So when is Ms. Fleming coming back?" Maria Lopez asked from the second row.

"Never, I hope," another girl said.

"What happened to the old bat?" I asked.

"She had a car accident," Jenna said, looking right at me. She looked *right* at me. I couldn't talk, I'm not even sure I was breathing.

"Is she dead?" some idiot football jock wanted to know.

"No, she's very much alive." Kirkland leaned against the desk and rolled his sleeves up to his elbows. He looked as if he wasn't used to the shirt-and-tie gig.

"Things could be better for her," he said. "She's in the hospital, and chances are I'll be your teacher for the rest of the school year."

"You give a lot of homework?" asked a kid who actually does homework.

I was still looking at Jenna—watching her listening to Kirkland. I wondered if she was checking him out, maybe getting a crush on him. He had that blond-haired, blue-eyed little boy look that girls like. I felt sick just thinking she was hot for him.

"Jenna," I whispered.

She looked at me but I didn't know what to say when she did. I shrugged my shoulders and looked behind me as if it had been somebody else calling her name. Mr. Smooth strikes again.

"Everybody introduced themselves at the start of class, but I didn't get to hear from you," Kirkland said to me. "You are?"

"Pip. Pip Downs."

"What a great name," he said. "Sounds like something out of an eighteenth-century British novel."

Jenna smiled when he said that. I wasn't sure if it was because she thought my name was cool or because she thought *he* was.

"I want to know what everyone's favorite book is," Kirkland said. "So let's start with you, Pip. What's the best book you've ever read?"

I was going to say something smart-ass to him about how I couldn't remember the last time I'd read a book. But he was smiling that old-pal smile at me and Jenna was waiting for my answer as if she really wanted to know what I was going to say.

"I forget what it was called. *The Outsiders* or something like that."

"S. E. Hinton. A great book. So you're a fan of stories with a lot of internal and external struggle—man against man, man against himself. The novel I'm assigning today is one of those."

He went on to bug somebody else. He didn't laugh at my answer and he didn't throw me out of class.

This was the first time since Ann Hutch Elementary that I had a teacher who didn't believe my rep—who didn't even know it.

This was wild. I was in class. I was awake. And Jenna was sitting next to me.

Not bad.

Kirkland passed out the books he wanted us to start. He said something about a quiz coming up, but I wasn't really listening. I was staring at the cover picture of two men—one all professor-looking and the other a monster. I'd seen a lot of cartoon spoofs of this story.

"'All human beings, as we meet them, are commingled out of good and evil,'" Kirkland quoted. "As you read the words in the book, read *between* them as well. See if you see yourself. See if you can determine the truth in those words as they apply to you or to those you know."

Jenna smiled at me. I didn't know why and I didn't care. I just soaked it up.

Maybe I'd read the book. It didn't sound too bad.

I shoved *Dr. Jekyll and Mr. Hyde* into my back pocket.

It was a perfect fit.

I remember swinging on the swings at the park.

I used to go so high that sometimes my butt would bounce off the leather strap.

It was as if I was flying.

When I showed up at Mikey's school, he was throwing rocks into that construction hole in front. His backpack was on the ground next to him.

"You got your mitt?" I asked him, hoping like hell I wasn't going to have to walk home to get it, then backtrack to the field for his stupid T-ball practice.

"Yeah, I got it in my pack." He tossed a rock down into the hole. "Listen," he said right before it clanked on something. His eyebrows went up as if it was the coolest thing in the world.

"Come on," I said, taking a gulp from the Coke can I had with me.

He picked up another rock and threw it up as high as he could in the air, letting it clunk to the bottom of the hole.

I picked up his backpack and started walking away, figuring he'd follow. When he caught up with me I shoved the backpack onto his shoulders.

"Pip?"

"What?"

"If you put M&M's in a bowl and put milk on it like cereal, what will happen?"

"The color will come off the shells and they'll get slimy."

"I want to try it."

We kept walking. Halfway to the field he said, "Pip? Guess what."

"What?" I took a drink from my Coke can.

"Daddy's coming on my class trip."

"Don't count on it."

"We're going to the zoo."

"You told me already."

"Daddy said he'd go."

"He was hungover when you were bugging him about it. He's not even going to remember he signed the permission slip."

"He promised."

"Even if he did, that doesn't mean he's going."

"You don't know everything."

"So stop *asking* me everything all the time."

He dropped his backpack when we got to the field, and started running off to his team.

"Mikey," I yelled, pulling his mitt out of the pack.

He turned around but kept running. I tossed the mitt up in the air to him. The little bugger caught it on the run and spiked it, shouting "Touchdown!"

Wrong sport.

I remember playing baseball with my father. He was trying to teach me how to pitch. Every boy in Little League wants to be the pitcher. But I wanted to be the catcher. I liked feeling the ball slam into the mitt.

My father kept having me practice my curveball. I hooked my wrist. I let it fly. I thought about what it would be like to say right out loud I don't want to pitch.

I wondered what it would be like to wear the catcher's mask.

I sat under a tree, away from all the parents watching their kids playing T-ball. I took a few slurps from my Coke can. The stupid paperback in my back pocket was digging into me. I lit a cigarette, then took a look at the book.

Dr. Jekyll and Mr. Hyde by Robert Louis Stevenson.

First line: "Mr. Utterson the lawyer was a man of a rugged countenance . . ."

Who's Utterson and what the hell does *countenance* mean? I wondered. But I kept reading. What else was I going to do? Watch T-ball?

Some guy in the book, Mr. Enfield, tried describing Hyde. "I never saw a man I so disliked, and yet I scarce know why."

More crap. I read a few pages of the book, but most of it didn't make any sense to me. "He was austere with himself; drank gin when he was alone . . ."

"Did you see me hit?" Mikey interrupted my reading, smiling all over his face as if it was Christmas morning.

"Not bad," I said, having no clue what he was talking about.

"Not bad? It was a home run!"

I hadn't been watching and I didn't need to feel like a shit about it either. Let his parents go to T-ball practice and yell rah-rah. Hell, at least I was there.

I'd smoked three cigarettes and almost finished the Coke. And I'd been reading the book and thinking the whole time. Wondering what this counseling thing was going to be like. Wondering how I was going to get the money to pay for my stash.

I pulled Mikey's backpack onto his shoulders and we started walking.

"Can I have a sip?" he asked when he saw me take a drink from the can.

I should have gotten him a Yoo-Hoo or something.

"No."

"I'm thirsty."

"No."

He put his hands around his neck, closed his eyes, and stuck his tongue out. "I'm real thirsty," he whined.

"We'll be home in a minute."

He grabbed my arm and the can spilled on me.

"Cut it out before I clobber you." I put the can to my mouth and finished what was left.

"I'm telling," he said.

"Telling who?" I crumpled the can in my hand and tossed it at a telephone pole.

"Ha ha. You missed," he said.

I should have brought him something to drink. I wasn't thinking about him.

All I thought about was getting to Slayer after school—getting some rum for my Coke.

Hey, I needed it.

Bugs didn't.

It was scary, though. First he eats my pot, then he tries to drink with me.

I didn't want to think about who this kid was going to be in ten years.

A line popped into my head right out of the Jekyll and Hyde book: *I let my brother go to the devil in his own way.*

He was heading there, all right. I just didn't want to think about it.

I want to know what to say to keep everybody off my back.

Maybe there's one word, one sentence. Hell, I'll even sing a song if I have to.

There was that song from when I was a kid about the monkeys jumping on the bed. I'll change the words. "Ten little monkeys jumpin' on my back. I pushed them off 'cause they didn't know jack. I smoked up some weed to get me some slack—here's more monkeys jumpin' on my back."

When Bugs and I got home, my mother was lying on the couch.

"I got to go somewhere," I told her. She didn't even turn around. All I saw was the back of her head and Mikey pulling on her arm, going on about his home run.

She did the old *that's nice, that's nice* thing to him that parents do when they're blowing you off. I had to get out of there. I'd done my job. I got him to T-ball. I got him home alive. Let him ask *her* a million questions about M&M's.

I stopped behind the deli. I had a couple of minutes to kill on my way to the counselor and needed some time to get myself right in the head. Hell, I was the best counselor I was ever going to have. I knew what I needed and I knew when. I needed a buzz. I needed something between me and the world, because the world was starting to feel like a pillow somebody was smashing into my face.

"Chimney Boy," Tony said, slamming his way out the back door of the deli. "I could use a toke. Pass it here." I didn't have much weed left and I wasn't looking to share it with the meat cutter.

"I don't charge you for grubbing my pot," I said. "Don't charge me for my next sandwich."

"This is your rent for planting your delinquent ass back here behind my job." He put his hand out and grabbed my blunt.

I let him get one hit, then took it out of his fingers. I sucked in as deep as I could.

"You sure are uptight, Chimney Boy," Tony said. He sat down on a milk crate and wiped his hands on his apron.

"I'm in a hurry."

"Where you headed?"

"Nowhere." I took another hit, and Tony reached his hand out again.

"I could have told you that. You're going nowhere faster than any kid I ever seen," he said, inhaling on the roach, then passing it back. "Your only hope is if a job opens up here at the deli and I'm stand-up enough to put in a good word for you."

I laughed. "Like I'm going to cut meat for a living."

"What do you think you're going to do? Trade stocks on Wall Street?"

I sucked in the last I could from the roach without burning my lip again.

"Go to hell," I told him, then dropped the roach on the ground and stepped on it.

"Already been, my friend. And you're on your way."

Maybe he was right. I was on my way to counseling—maybe I *was* on my way to hell.

I remember when I was a little kid and I wanted to grow up to be a car mechanic.

I liked the idea of lying under cars and getting dirty. I could roll out from under the car on that board with wheels, and roll back under again whenever I didn't want anybody to find me.

The waiting room was the size of my parents' walk-in closet. There were plenty of pamphlets for me to read if I wanted to know more about sexually transmitted diseases. But who wants to know about the hundred different rashes they could get on their privates? There was another pamphlet on the dangers of steroid use. Only dumb jocks need to read that one, but they can't read anyway. My favorite pamphlet was *Talking With Your Kids About Drugs and Alcohol*. It was way too late for that one. Besides, there should be one for talking to your *parents* about drugs and alcohol.

There were a few stupid signs hanging on the wall. No Smoking (no smoking what?); In Case of Fire Follow These Instructions (yeah, get the hell out as fast as you can); and We Appreciate the Referrals of Your Family and Friends (thanks for letting us make even more money off your problems).

There was a kid about Mikey's age sitting next to his mother. She was flipping through *People* magazine and he was making shooting sounds with his action figure.

Another boy who looked about six walked in with two smaller kids crying and fighting behind him. A woman came in with them, carrying a bag that took up half the room. It was too crowded in there. I was getting ready to walk out when the counselor came from down the hall.

"Pip?" she asked, smiling at me.

What a genius. I was the only sixteen-year-old guy standing there.

She was wearing this long skirt down to her ankles, a big blouse with flowers all sewn into it, and about eight million beads around her neck. She had four earrings in each ear. Her hair was all short and spiked and looked as if she never combed the gel out of it.

I'd guessed that Claire Butler was going to be like any other school counselor or teacher I'd ever met. Older than my mother, ugly, and with a voice that could cut glass with some *you'd better straighten up* speech. But she was kind of young and didn't look like anybody I'd ever seen in an office anywhere.

But she was still a counselor. She was still on Giraldi's side. She was one of them and she wasn't getting a piece of me.

She sort of waved her hand for me to follow her, so I did. Her office was even smaller than the waiting room. I sat down on some low green chair, feeling like my butt was on the ground. I pushed back with my feet until the chair hit the wall behind me. I didn't want to be too close to her, but no matter where I sat, I would be.

"Where'd you get this chair?" I asked. "A garage sale for circus midgets?"

Her desk was against the wall with her chair facing it. She turned the chair to face me instead, and sat down. But she couldn't sit still. Her chair had wheels, and she kept swiveling back and forth on it. I felt like asking her if she was on speed or something.

"You coming in for a landing?" I said instead.

"Am I making you dizzy?"

"Not really. I got other people for that."

She smiled. "So, Pip. Welcome. It's nice to meet you. How about we start with you telling me why you're here."

"I had an appointment," I said.

I looked around her office at all the dumb stuff she had. There were a few you-can-do-it kind of posters on the wall, some little statues, and one of those plastic framed prayers you could get at any Hallmark store: *God grant me the serenity . . .*

She was probably some religious freak who was going to bang a tambourine and tell me how Jesus saves and drugs kill.

"I know that Mr. Giraldi wanted you to begin counseling," she said. "But I want to know why you decided to come."

"He blackmailed me. He said if I didn't come he was going to have me killed."

Her eyebrows went up.

"So here's what I was thinking. You tell him I'm coming. I stay alive, and you get an hour off without having to counsel anybody. You could read a book—do your nails."

"That wouldn't work."

"Why not?"

"It comes out to more than one hour a week. One time you come in on your own, and two times a week you're here in group."

"What the hell is group?"

"A bunch of high school guys come in. We all talk—bounce some ideas around. They're trying to change some things in their lives."

"I wouldn't fit in with your group."

"Why not?"

"I'm not trying to change anything."

"Your life is fine."

"My life sucks. I'm just not looking to change it."

"Because you don't know how."

"Because I don't see the point."

"Your life sucks but you want it to stay that way?"

"Nothing's going to change in my life because I sit here bitchin' to you about it. I know that much."

"Then you know a lot. You're right. Bitching doesn't change anything. You do."

I looked around for a clock and couldn't find one.

"My time up yet?"

"No. Why? You in a hurry?"

"I already told you. I don't want to be here."

"So leave."

"I can't."

"Sure you can."

"No, I can't. If I don't come when you tell me to, I get expelled."

"So then you *want* to be here."

I was really starting to think she was on something.

"I *have* to be here."

"Let's get something straight. You don't have to be here. You're responsible for your own choices, including any choices you made that got you in this predicament. If you want to stay in school you have to come here. So, whether or not it's your first choice of how you spend your time, you do want to come here."

"Is my time up?"

"What do *you* think you want, Pip?" She stopped rocking the chair and waited for me to answer.

"I want to get out of here."

"What else? What do you really want in life?"

I want my own pizza—the whole pie. Double cheese.

I took a cigarette out of my pack and put it between my lips. I was waiting for her to tell me I couldn't smoke. She didn't say anything. I guess she knew I wasn't going to light it.

"So what do you want, Pip?"

"Nothin'."

"Maybe you just don't know what you want."

"Maybe you just don't listen. I told you I want to get out of here."

"Are you committed to the counseling or not?"

"I have no choice."

"You have nothing but choices."

What I really wanted was a joint. If she let me light up right there, I could have stayed without giving too much of a crap. The whole thing was making my head spin.

"So let's talk about the drug part."

How did she know what I was thinking?

"Mr. Giraldi said he thinks you have a pretty hefty habit— that that's why you sleep in class and get into the trouble that you do."

"Maybe you should just talk to him. Sounds like you think he knows everything."

"Well, you're not giving up much here. *You* tell me. How big is your habit?"

"I don't do drugs. I'm a health nut."

"Right, and herbs are an integral part of your diet." She swiveled in the chair a few times. "If you can get honest from the beginning, we won't have to waste a lot of time. We can get right to helping you out."

"You think I'm lying?" I took the butt out of my mouth.

"I can tell you're stoned right now." She said this with a straight face. "Your pupils are so dilated, I could throw a Frisbee through one eye and watch it fly out the other."

I pulled my lips into my mouth, trying real hard not to smile.

"You smell like a giant burning stick of reefer."

"How do you know what reefer smells like?" I asked her.

"Aha," she said with her eyebrows going up.

"'Aha' what?"

"That's a trick question."

"You ever smoke weed or not?"

"If I tell you I have, you'll point to me and say, *See? I can do it too. You turned out fine.* If I say I never smoked it, you'll tell me I don't understand you."

I put my cigarette back in the pack. "I don't really care anyway," I said.

"Good. I'd rather talk about you. Ever try to go a day without it?"

"Without what?"

"Come on, Pip. I can smell the pot. Hell, the birds outside who got a whiff of you are still enjoying their buzz."

"Is my time up?"

"Almost. But if you're going along with counseling, you need to be back tomorrow at four o'clock for group."

"Who's in this group?"

"Four guys, fifteen to seventeen years old."

"No girls?"

"I have a separate group for the girls. I don't need you all distracting each other."

"What do you do in group?"

"Talk—mostly about what they're trying to change and what's hard about doing it."

"So what do *they* want?"

"You'll have to ask *them*." She opened a desk drawer and pulled out a Dixie cup. "How about a urine sample?" she asked, handing me the cup.

"No, thanks. I just had a soda."

"The bathroom is right next door."

"Why do I have to do this?"

"Anyone receiving counseling here is subject to periodic drug testing. It helps us obtain information that would otherwise be avoided or lied about."

"What?"

"If you don't pee in the cup, you can't come here."

I opened her office door and started to walk to the bathroom.

"You should get a clock in your office," I told her. "So a guy knows how much time he has left to get tortured."

"You could wear a watch," she said.

Bitch.

I want to land my playing piece back on Go.

You know, like when you're a little kid playing a game and something goes wrong. Everybody yells, Do over!

I want that—a do-over.

■　■　■

"Thanks for the eats," I said to Johnny.

We were sitting in one of the booths at Mia Pizza Amore. I'd caught up with him at the Site after seeing the counselor. He was hungry. I was hungry. We both hate eating at home. So we split a pie.

"No problem. I made a lot of money today."

"You started selling?"

"Hell, yeah. You need to get in on this. I can't keep up. An hour after my first buyer walked away I had almost every jock, cheerleader, and pothead bugging me for weed."

We tossed our garbage into the pail and went outside. It was already dark and getting cool out. I lit a cigarette and handed my last one to Johnny.

"I got two bags in my jacket right now with your name on them," he said. "One is for you to sell, the other is all yours to smoke."

"That's a lot of grass."

"I got two full bottles of ecstasy you can sell too if you want. And in a couple of days there's a bag of coke coming my way. We sell that and the weed, you'll have enough money to take your little brother to Disneyland."

He took off his jacket and shook it onto my shoulders. "Borrow this tonight," he said. "The bags are in the pockets. Listen, if you're going to do this with me, you got to wear your own jacket or carry a backpack or something so I can pass stuff to you. This time tomorrow *you'll* be paying for our pizza." He flicked his cigarette butt into the street with a stupid-looking grin on his face. "And tie your damn shoes. You're going to trip and drop the goods."

"Yeah, and zip your fly," I told him. "You're going to drop your brain."

He grabbed his crotch, gave me the finger, then took off down the street.

I slapped the top pocket of his jacket and felt one of the bags stuffed there.

I wasn't thinking about selling.

I was thinking about smoking.

I want a new drug.
It has to be easy to get.
It has to be free.
It has to work.

"Want to play winner?" my father asked me.

He was lying on the floor with Mikey and a checkerboard. They had a bowl of Cheez Doodles next to them. Mikey was sucking on the straw of a fruit punch juice-box. My father had a glass in his hand—big surprise.

Mikey made a muscle. "I won all six games. I'm king of checkers."

Dad winked at me.

"Where's Mom?" I asked.

"She went to bed," my father said. "She was pretty tired."

"Sounds good." I opened the refrigerator and grabbed myself a can of ginger ale. "Good night," I said.

"Wait a second. Hang out with us a little bit." My father got up off the floor and came over to me. "What have you been up to?"

"I had some stuff to do."

He nodded his head as if he thought maybe I was going to

tell him more than that. I didn't—just started walking to the stairs so I could get to my room.

"Let's talk about a time we can get you on the road, give you a driving lesson."

Mr. Talk-About-It-and-Never-Do-It.

"How about right now," I said, knowing he wasn't even going to think about it.

"It's dark," he said with a smile. "Can't go out your first time in the dark."

"Whatever. You let me know when."

I was hoping Mikey was paying attention to the promise game my father likes so much. The one he always wins, while everybody else is left standing around wondering why the hell they ever bothered playing along.

"What's this?" he asked, pulling the book out of my pocket.

I grabbed it back. "Homework I got to do. I'm going up to my room to read it."

"Good for you," he said, and gave me an old-pal shot in the arm. "Buckle down. Get those grades up."

I looked over at Mikey. He was setting the checkers up again.

"Come on, Dad," he said around a mouthful of Cheez Doodles.

I couldn't get away from my father fast enough. He does this flip-flop thing all the time. One minute he wants to play a game, the next minute you *are* game.

Mikey will catch on someday.

"That's not your jacket," Bugs said when I was walking away.

"Shut up," I said.

■ ■ ■

I remember getting a five-speed bike for my ninth birthday.

I kept leaving it in the driveway. My father kept telling me if I didn't learn to park it in the garage or out back, he was putting it in the trash.

One morning the garbagemen were outside our house. They always dump the garbage, then toss the pails down the driveway. But that morning they were standing around talking about whether or not to put my bike in the front with the driver or try to tie it to the side of the truck.

It was too nice a bike to trash.

Anybody could see that.

I had two full bags of pot. That never happened.

These weren't just the small bags you buy from a kid at school—ones with enough pot inside to roll five to ten joints. These were bags I could turn into twenty of those smaller bags. That's either a lot of money to be made or a lot of partying to be done.

I shoved one in the back of my closet inside an old boot. The other one I opened.

I put my nose to the edge of the plastic and sniffed. If I smoked the whole thing right there I could have had a buzz that lasted a week—maybe two. That would have made for a decent vacation from my life, from my head. Sounded good to me.

The pictures in my head were going crazy. The cop bringing me home; my mother's face that morning; my father promising for the hundredth time to give me a driving lesson; Claire telling me I had nothing but choices.

Then I did something I told myself I'd never do. I lit up right there in my room.

I got a pack of rolling paper out of my dresser drawer, and

rolled myself a thick, perfect number. I opened the window and put the top part of my body outside. While I lit the joint I took in the deepest inhale of my life.

Everything was quiet outside except for some crickets doing a rock and roll concert. It was like nothing was moving anywhere on the street.

I blew the smoke out into the dark and took another long hit.

I was starting to feel as still as everything else outside.

I was starting to feel like myself again.

Nobody in the house was going to know what I was doing. Nobody was looking for me.

But I'd never chanced it before. If my parents caught me getting high, my mother wouldn't want me anywhere near my brother. My father wouldn't want me around ever again. They'd run my ass to a rehab so far from home, I'd never find my way back.

But that night I didn't care. I wasn't even thinking about all the stuff I was afraid of. All I knew was that I had more pot on me than ever. I had a ton.

The bag had been calling my name, begging me to smoke it. I could have gone back to the Site or even just down the block to light up. But I couldn't wait.

I couldn't wait.

The rules didn't matter, and anyway, the only ones left for me to break were my own.

I want a photo album.

Then I could take all the pictures in my head, put them in the album, and close it.

■ ■ ■

"Pip, wake up."

Mikey was pulling on my arm. I was in bed, still in my clothes in one of the deepest sleeps of my life. That wasn't just pot Johnny gave me. That was Super Pot. That was supreme number one ultimate stuff.

"Go away," I told Bugs, and rolled over.

"I hear them," he whispered in my ear.

"Hear what?"

"Beasties."

I rubbed my eyes and tried to get a look at my brother in the dark. He was wearing his red Superman cape and had his pillow under his arm.

"There's beasties. Outside. I hear them in the garage."

"There's no such thing as beasties."

If I had a dollar for every time I'd said that to him, I'd have enough money for a year's supply of weed.

I got up off the bed and stuck my head out the window. "There's nothing out there—"

"Listen." The kid looked as if he'd just seen a ghost.

Then I heard it. I heard a bang, then a sound like something falling.

I stuck my head back out the window. Mikey was right. Somebody was coming out of the garage.

It was the Grinch, on his way into the house.

"Go to your room," I told Mikey. "I'll get you in a few minutes."

I started to pull my boots on and heard the front door slam downstairs.

"Go to your room," I told him again.

Something was about to go down and he didn't have to be around for it.

"I don't want the beasties to get me." His lip was shaking.

Footsteps were stomping up the stairs. Mikey was too late to make a getaway.

"It's not a beastie, Bugs. It's Dad."

I don't think that made him feel any better.

My bedroom door slammed open into the wall behind it. Mikey jumped.

"Let's go, mister," the Grinch yelled at me.

"I know. You want me to go out at"—I looked at the time on my alarm clock—"twelve thirty-two and clean the garage. Right?"

"I wanted you to do it when I told you to. So, yes, you have to do it now at twelve thirty-two at night."

"Come on, Mikey." I gave the kid a little push to get him out of the room—to get him away from the Grinch.

"You're not going anywhere," he said, grabbing the collar of Mikey's pajama top. "You're going to read that book the teacher sent home for you to read."

"I read it already," Mikey said, two bowls of water filling up in his eyes.

"Are you trying to be like your brother over here—not listening to me?"

"Give him a break," I said.

"I told you to get outside, Mr. Wise Guy."

Mikey looked lost. He squeezed his pillow into his stomach and blinked real hard. "But Dad, I read the book to you tonight—before bed. Two times."

"Don't argue with me. Get the book now!" Dad screamed so

loud at the kid, I thought a vein was going to bust out of his neck.

"*The Happy Duck,*" Mikey said. He was looking at our father as if he was crazy.

"Come on, Mikey," I said. "Just get the book."

I started to push him out of my room with me, but he turned around and kept talking. "Duck can run. Duck ran and ran. Duck was fun. Duck—"

"See?" My father was smirking. "You never read it. You just memorized the whole thing so it would *look* like you were reading."

"What's your problem?" I asked the Grinch, and pushed Mikey out the door some more.

"I did so read it," Mikey argued.

"Get another book from your room—one with some big words in it," my father said. "Then we'll see if you really know how to read."

I gave Mikey a hard shove into the hall and slammed my bedroom door shut behind us. He was doing to Mikey the same kind of crappy thing he did to me when I was that age. The only difference was that even back then I knew the guy was crazy.

Mikey didn't.

He was still trying to reason with the man—make him see.

I remember lying under my bed with my hands over my ears.

I knew my father was looking for me.

He'd told me I was too stupid to tie my own shoes.

I went into his closet and tied knots, big knots, on every pair of shoes he had.

I figured he was the one who was stupid. He wasn't going to be able to untie my knots.

"Just get the book for him," I told Mikey. "He's never going to let up on you."

I started to go down the stairs.

"Where are you going?" he asked.

"I have to clean the friggin' garage." I kept walking.

I heard him following me.

"Bugs, you have to stay upstairs and get the book or he's going to kill you."

"Kill me?"

Crap. I shouldn't have said it like that.

"I mean he's going to kick your butt if you don't do what he says."

My bedroom door opened and the Grinch came flying out. He grabbed Mikey by the back of his pajamas and lifted him up off the floor.

"Hey," I yelled, and watched while the fat bastard threw my brother into his room. For a second it looked as if Mikey really could fly, with his cape flapping behind him.

"Get the book!" Dad screamed. "Now."

"You want to throw somebody," I yelled back, "throw me!" Then I went toe-to-toe with the only person I've ever really been afraid of.

He grabbed the front of my T-shirt, and I slammed the palms of my hands into his chest.

"Stop it!" my mother yelled, coming up the stairs. Where the hell was she when this all got started? Did she know he'd been prowling around in the garage? Did she know he'd run upstairs to throw his sons around? Did she know it was after friggin' midnight? Did she have any clue how to keep her damn husband on a leash?

The punch came out of nowhere. At least it felt that way. I knew he was going to hit me. I just wasn't thinking a left hook to my right eye.

I fell back against the wall and put my hands over my face. Bugs came running out of his room still holding his pillow—still wearing his cape—and crushed his body against mine.

"Stop it!" my mother yelled again.

My father was yelling back at her about what a wiseass I am and how my brother was no better than me and probably on his way to turning out worse.

The way I saw it, I was getting crap because I'd ducked out of cleaning the garage and because I always get crap.

Mikey was getting in trouble just for being with me—just for being my brother.

I remember when I was ten and Mikey was two days old.

"It's an important job being a big brother," my mother told me. She was lying in bed with the baby's head under her nightgown.

"Why?" I asked.

"He's going to need you to watch out for him."

"Why?"

"The world isn't always a friendly place."

I put my hand on Mikey's shoulder and moved him in front of me down the stairs.

"Michael Junior, get back here," the Grinch yelled. "I told you to bring me that book."

I hurried Mikey downstairs even faster, and when we got to the bottom I picked him up and carried him through the kitchen and out the door. As soon as I put him down, he ran to the garage door. I lifted it up and he ran under. I ducked in too, then let the door fall back down behind me. I turned the lock handle, pulled the light chain hanging from the ceiling, and waited.

Mikey and I were both out of breath. He was shaking. I was sweating.

I heard the front door slam. I double-checked the garage door lock.

Behind me, boxes were knocked over and some of the nail jars were smashed. My father isn't a bar-brawling, get-pulled-over-for-a-DWI kind of drunk. He's just the throw-shit-around-the-house and make-your-family-scared-to-death-of-you kind.

The lock handle jiggled. Then he started banging on the door. Mikey ran to the back of the garage.

"What are you doing in there? Having a tea party?" He kicked the door. "Unlock this."

"What for?" I yelled back. My hands were shaking. My eye hurt like hell. "So you can hit me upside the head again?"

"Fine. Stay in there all night then. Sleep on the damn concrete. Just don't come out until that garage is clean."

I heard him walk away. The front door opened and slammed shut again.

I turned around and looked at the mess. How the hell was I ever going to clean it? It was like telling a man with no tools to build a house—in one night.

I felt like I was going to throw up. I tried to push it away by taking a deep breath. My eye was stinging, and even though I was sweating, I was cold.

I looked for my brother but didn't see him anywhere. "Mikey? Bugs?"

I saw his foot. He was hiding under the counter in the back of the garage.

I bent down and pulled him out from behind the lawn mower. He had snot on his lip, and there was a puddle on the ground where he'd been.

"He's in the house, Bugs," I said.

He stood up—shaking and crying. "What's going to happen now?"

Another one of his crazy questions I couldn't answer.

I pulled down the toboggan that was hanging on the wall. I wiped the dust off of it with my hand and put Mikey's pillow on one end.

"I'm going to clean the garage," I told him. "And *you* are going to sleep."

"I don't want to."

"We're going to be in here all night, Bugs. So you should just go to sleep."

"I can help you clean."

"Come here." I pushed the sled against the wall and sat on it. He sat next to me.

"I got to do this thing in here. I want you to sleep so I don't have to carry you to school tomorrow."

He stared at me real hard. I wasn't sure what he was looking at. Then he touched my eye where I'd been hit.

"Does it hurt?" he asked.

"Not too bad," I said, and stood up. "Lie down."

He put his head on the pillow and shoved his thumb in his mouth. I grabbed a handful of plastic bags out of the box on the counter. The only way I was going to clean the garage was by throwing out a lot of stuff. And I needed to move fast so I could get some sleep too.

I filled a couple of garbage bags with junk. I didn't care what I was tossing or whose it was. It wasn't my problem anymore. The garbagemen could take it all, just like they took my bike when I was a kid.

"Pip?"

"What?"

"You still keep kryptonite in your pocket?"

Hiding in the garage, I figured I wasn't looking too tough to him.

"Go to sleep, Bugs."

"Pip. Come here."

I went over to where he was lying. He waved his hand for me to bend over, then took the cape off his neck and shoved it in the back of my T-shirt.

It was like he was thinking I was some kind of hero.

Poor kid.

I took it off and put it on the end of the sled.

I want to take a nap.
For about ten years.

"Pip?"

"Try to go to sleep, Mikey."

"What about the beasties?" he asked me.

I was going to tell him again that there was no such thing as beasties.

But I didn't want to lie to the kid.

"They're sleeping," I told him. "Now you go to sleep too."

I didn't look back at him while I was cleaning. I tried not to hear him either. I tried not to hear how hard he was sucking on his thumb. I tried not to hear him crying. I just kept throwing stuff in bags. Everything that didn't look like anything I'd ever care about went: my father's tools, Christmas decorations, papers, magazines, shelves. It all went.

I didn't have a watch on. I had no idea what time it was or how long I'd been throwing stuff out. Before I knew it I'd used the whole box of garbage bags. There had to be twenty-five of them stuffed and piled up next to the door.

There were some boxes I'd left in the back. They looked like stuff my mother had packed and was saving. I didn't want to trash anything that might mean something to her.

I was tired. I was dog-ass tired.

I sat down next to the sled and caught a look at my brother. He was sleeping with his thumb in his mouth. He can be sort of cute when he's not shooting his mouth off.

I took the cape off the sled and put it over him like a blanket.

Poor little guy—sleeping in the garage on top of a sled wearing wet pajamas. He had nothing to hold on to but his thumb and the thought that someday he'd fly like Superman.

At least I could get high.

I pulled up my sock to see if I had a joint.

Nothin'.

I'd left the kryptonite in my bedroom.

I want to know what my little brother is going to be like in ten years. On second thought, I don't want to know.

The tapping on the garage door woke me up.

I was on the floor, leaning against the toboggan with my head on Mikey's leg. I stood up, walked over to the door, and listened.

"What?" I asked.

"It's Mom. Open up."

I looked over at Bugs. I didn't want to wake him by pulling the door open.

"What time is it?"

"Five-thirty," she said.

I rubbed my eyes like I always do when I wake up. My right eye stung.

"Come back and get us up in an hour," I told her.

"You can't sleep in there all night."

"Where've you been, Mom? We already did."

"He knew I was going to come out for you. He wouldn't let me leave," she said. "I waited for him to fall asleep, but I ended up falling asleep first."

Big surprise.

"Come out of there," she said. "Before your father wakes up."

"Is that why you're here?" I banged the side of my head against the garage door and left it there. "You don't want Dad to wake up and remember what an asshole he was last night. You want us to come in and play make-believe with you—pretend we're all one big happy family."

She's crazy.

"I don't want everything starting up again," she said.

Unbelievable. "You think you can stop it?"

I was probably having the longest talk with my mother that

I'd ever had, and she was standing on one side of a wall with me on the other.

Figures.

"Get your brother inside," she said.

I picked my head up off the door. "He's okay right here," I said.

I looked over at him. He wasn't okay. Neither of us was.

But we didn't really have a choice.

I could hear Claire in my head saying, *You have nothing* but *choices.*

Yeah. She was going to be a lot of help. She didn't know a thing about my life—about me.

"Come back in an hour," I said again and walked to the other end of the garage. I knew I wouldn't be able to hear her tapping on the door or walking away from back there.

I remember the first day of kindergarten.

My mother walked me to school—stopped at the front door and kissed me on the cheek before sending me in.

"Work hard," she said.

"You coming back?" I asked.

"Don't worry about that."

But I did. All day.

"Do your work," she said. "Learn a lot."

She didn't tell me how much I'd have to learn for her to come back—what I'd have to know for her to walk me past the door.

There was no way I was going to fall asleep again. I wasn't even going to try.

I sat on the counter in the back of the garage, banging my feet into the boxes I'd left there.

Something was digging into my butt. It was the Jekyll and Hyde book from English class. I read it for a little while.

"It seems scarcely a house. There is no other door, and nobody goes in or out of that one, but, once in a great while, the gentleman of my adventure."

I stared at the garage door. Pictures of my father started going through my head. I thought about how he was one person at his job, never yelling at anybody—and somebody else at home who could scream so loud, the windows shook.

I thought about his potion bottles all lined up on top of the refrigerator. He drank his potion—his scotch—and most of the time when he did, he turned into his own kind of monster.

Dad. The Grinch. The Beastie.

Hyde.

I put the book down and jumped off the counter. My eye hurt. I was cold. I was hungry. I was tired. I was angry. I needed something to get the edge off. I was dying for a joint.

All I could think to do was look in the boxes by my feet. I knew I wouldn't find any food or pot in them. But it would kill time until my mother came back to get us up for school.

The first box had those statues of my mother's in it. The second box was full of photos. There were 4x7's, 3x5's, old school mug shots, and a ton of family pictures.

I grabbed a handful and looked through them. In some, Mom looked real young—not a single gray hair like the ones I'd been seeing lately. She was even smiling in a few of them. But I guess people are supposed to do that for pictures. There were pictures of Mom and me, Mikey and me, Mikey and me with

Mom. There were pictures of my father with his father, with Mikey, with Mom, with both of them.

I kept pulling pictures out of the box. Searching. I was doing it so fast, I finally dumped the damn thing over and poured them all out on the floor. I couldn't find one. There wasn't even one picture of me with my father.

Not one.

Screw him.

I started to shove the pictures back into the box. I was going to put them away, wake Mikey, and get ready for another messed-up day.

Then I saw it.

It was a picture my mother had taken the first day I learned how to ride a two-wheeler without training wheels.

My father had his arm around my shoulder. He was pulling me into his side and smiling.

I remembered that day. I was psyched I'd ridden the bike, but I was pissed too. He'd promised he wouldn't let go of the back of the bike without telling me, but he did. He told me he had to let go—it was the only way I was going to learn. He said he knew I wasn't going to fall.

"Get up, Mikey." I pulled open the garage door, hoping it was loud enough to wake my father—hoping he had a hangover and that I was making it worse.

"What's going on?" Mikey asked, sitting up and looking around.

"You're not dreaming, Bugs. You slept in the garage last night."

I started dragging the bags to the end of the driveway. I wanted the garbagemen to get them before my father had a chance to go through them.

Mikey grabbed one with both hands and started dragging it.

"Go inside," I told him. "I'll do this. Get dressed, eat breakfast, and we'll get out of here quick this morning."

"Okay."

He went into the garage, grabbed his pillow and his cape, and ran back to the house.

"Pip?" he said when he got to the door.

"What?"

"Don't tell anybody. Okay?"

"Tell anybody what?"

He rolled his eyes and kept his teeth together so he was just talking through his lips. "That I wet my pants."

I dragged three bags at once down the driveway. "I don't know what you're talking about," I said.

He ran inside, yelling out a "Thanks" on the way in.

After I got all the bags out, I went into the house and up to my room. I got my stash, rolled a joint, grabbed a book of matches, and went back outside.

I didn't go far, just down the street behind the house of some old people. I figured they'd never hear me out there.

I lit up.

My eye still hurt. I was still hungry and tired and pissed.

But after a few hits I just didn't care anymore.

Nothing mattered.

THREE

I want to go someplace where nobody can find me.
Not even me.

I walked Mikey to school, and told him that I was going to drop him off at Eddie's house later.

"Okay," he said. He didn't put up a fight or whine this time. Smart kid.

"How's your eye?" he asked.

"I put some ice on it—"

"Dad say anything?"

"What do you think?"

"Mom?"

"Nobody said a word, Bugs. Nobody ever does after something like last night."

"Mom asked me if I was okay," he said.

"What did you tell her?"

"I said I was fine."

"So you lied?"

"I don't know. I guess."

We crossed the street to his school. All the other kids were laughing, trading baseball cards, tossing footballs. They didn't look tired like my little brother. He didn't look so much like a kid that morning. He looked different.

He was probably the only kid in his school who woke up on a toboggan in his garage.

"See ya later, Bugs."

"Listen to this," he said.

He took his time finding just the right rock off the ground, then he threw it up as high as he could, letting out a grunt when he did.

"Hear that?" he asked when it clanked. "The higher it goes, the harder it falls when it hits the bottom."

I remember when I was a kid and I'd run around the house shutting all the windows so the neighbors wouldn't hear my dad yelling.

Yeah.

I remember when I used to care what other people thought.

"What happened to you?" Jenna asked as soon as I walked into class.

I didn't know what she was talking about. I sat down in the seat next to her.

"You didn't get that at the party the other night. It would have shown up yesterday."

"What?"

Then she touched me.

She put her fingers under my right eye and left her hand there a couple of seconds. I thought my whole body was turning into oatmeal. I couldn't talk.

"Who punched you in the eye?"

"Oh—that."

"You get into a lot of fights, don't you?"

"Not really—"

"Well, you didn't do it yourself," she said.

Then Kirkland came in and started right up about the Jekyll and Hyde book.

I didn't listen. I was too busy looking at Jenna. I was watching the side of her face—the way her eyes were following Kirkland as he walked around the room. The way she flipped her hair off her shoulder. Her eyes were smiling even though her mouth wasn't. I thought that was a cool trick.

"Pip," Kirkland said. He was leaning his hands on my desk. "When Jekyll turns into Hyde, he becomes smaller in stature. Why do you think Hyde is smaller than Jekyll?"

I didn't know what to say. I figured I wasn't far enough in the book to know what he was talking about.

I took my best shot and tried making a joke out of it. "I guess maybe 'cause Hyde is hiding."

A couple of people in the class cracked up. They do that a lot when I say stuff—even when I'm not trying to be funny. It doesn't bother me because I could always kick their asses later.

Kirkland pulled back from my desk and crossed his arms. "That really wasn't the answer I was looking for," he said.

I figured.

"It's got me thinking, though. It reminds me of a line in the book where I believe it's Utterson who says, 'If he be Mr. Hyde I shall be Mr. Seek.' We're meant to consider that the evil that exists within each of us is only a small part of who we are. No matter how big and ugly the evil may seem, in reality it's only a smaller, crouching version of our true selves. It is not who we are. Jekyll is not Hyde. But he has a part of him that, as Pip points out, is hiding."

I said that?

I remember this time once when I was nine and my father was watching a Yankee game. He had six empty beer bottles next to him on the coffee table. I couldn't figure out why it wasn't called a beer table.

He told me to get him another one from the fridge.

I did. I took a sip from it too. I wanted to see what the big deal was.

"You slobbered on this?" he asked me.

"I wanted to taste it," I told him.

"You did, huh? Fine then. You sit right here now until you finish the whole bottle."

So I did.

It didn't help me figure out what the big deal was.

I thought my first beer tasted like piss.

I checked the clock. It was time to go.

I got a hall pass from Kirkland so I could go to the bathroom. The hall was empty—everybody was in class pretending to listen. I caught up with Slayer just when he got to his locker.

"What's going on?" he asked.

"Nothin'. Just trying to get through the day without killing somebody."

He took a swig from the Snapple bottle behind his jacket. He handed it to me, and I looked up and down the hall, then took two long pulls from it.

"I don't know how you're doing it, man," Slayer said as he took back the bottle. "I could never make it to every class—I'd go nuts."

"This helps," I said, taking another slug from the bottle, the alcohol hitting the back of my throat in a way that hurt real good.

"So what the hell happened to your face?"

"My eye? I got it banging my damn head against the wall."

"You get into a fight?"

"Not exactly," I said.

He knew what I meant. "Don't sweat it, man. Meet us at the Site after school. Johnny sold some weed to a couple of girls who want to hang out with us."

"What girls?"

"I don't know—Sharon something and Alison somebody."

"You selling for Johnny?"

"I'm selling with him. He thinks if he gives me a bag to sell on my own, I'll smoke it all."

I took another drink and told Slayer I had to get going.

I walked back into class with my best *everything's cool* look on my face.

"Pip," Kirkland said, putting his hands on my desk again as I sat down. "Why do you suppose Jekyll drank the potion to begin with?"

Good question. I shook my head.

"Can't hear you," he said.

"I don't know."

He took his hands off my desk and stepped back. He asked somebody else the same question and that kid had no idea either.

The bell rang.

I was thinking of what I was going to say to Jenna—how I could maybe get her to touch my face again.

"Pip," Kirkland said, "can I see you?"

Damn.

I went over to his desk as everybody else walked out. I looked for Jenna, but she was already gone.

"That was an excellent answer you gave in class today," he said.

"Thanks."

"Are you enjoying the book?"

"It's okay."

"As far as books go, right?"

"Right."

"I find the whole concept of the potion really interesting."

That's nice, I'm thinking, but I gotta get to my next class.

"We all have our thing we turn to so we can cut loose. I turn my stereo up way too loud when I'm driving sometimes."

What a dangerous, on-the-edge kind of guy.

"Some people eat a lot, some gamble, some even drink a potion they can buy at the mini-mart."

"The bell's going to ring—"

"I'll give you a late pass." He crossed his arms and leaned back against his desk. "Everything all right, Pip?"

"What are you talking about?"

"The black eye, the alcohol on your breath when you came back from the bathroom?"

Damn. Couldn't blame this one on wood shop.

"You okay?" he asked.

"A kid I know was passing a bottle around the bathroom. I took one sip—"

"But are you okay?"

"I'm fine." I looked at the clock.

"Don't ask for a bathroom pass in my class anymore," he said.

"Sure."

I got off easy.

He handed me a late pass, and I started to walk out.

"Pip," he said, "your laces are untied."

I didn't want to shoot my mouth off to him. If he sent me to Giraldi, my father would be getting that phone call.

"Yeah, thanks," I said, and walked out.

I remember the first time I got high.

I was eleven.

I was at Johnny's apartment playing Nintendo with him. His mother had left one of her bags of pot out on the table. Johnny opened it and rolled a number.

He said he knew how from watching her do it.

He lit it, took a hit, then handed it to me.

I think it was the first deep breath I ever took.

I didn't just smoke that joint—I made it a part of me.

Mikey was dragging ass on our walk to Eddie's house. I had to slow down a couple of times so he could catch up.

"What's going on with you?" I asked him.

"Nothin'," he said. Then he asked me, "Do I have to go to Eddie's today?"

"Yeah, you have to go."

"I don't want to. I want to stay with you."

"You'll have a better time with Eddie than you would hanging with me."

"No I won't. Let me come. I won't bug you."

"No."

"I just want to go home. I want to be with you."

"Shut up already. You're going to Eddie's."

I didn't look at him again for the rest of the walk. I left him on Eddie's front step and lit a cigarette while I listened to him go inside. I really didn't need his kind of crap with everything else I had going on.

I ran all the way to the Site, thinking about the four joints I had lined up in my sock. I was hoping I could smoke two or three of them before going to Claire's stupid group.

Johnny and Slayer were already there with four girls. They were all smoking and drinking and laughing. Johnny was leaning against Hahn's headstone, holding a joint to one of the girls' lips. Slayer was kissing another girl next to Agnes Jaffe. I wondered if I'd ever get Jenna to come to the Site.

I lit up and put my head back on Beattie's headstone.

"Pip," Johnny said, "grab a beer, some chips and cookies. We're having a party."

I tossed him his jacket.

"Do any business today?" he asked me.

I shook my head, and got into the drinking and smoking and eating. I don't remember too much about it.

I do know that I forgot all about the pictures in my head. All that stuff left me alone for a little while. Nothing was bothering me. I wasn't feeling any pain. I wasn't feeling anything.

I didn't even care when Johnny told me he was going to give me a matching shiner for my other eye if he didn't see some money for all the weed he'd given me. He was too wasted to punch me. He'd never do it anyway.

"Is it four-fifteen yet?" I asked about a hundred times.

"What the hell are you in a panic about?" Slayer asked.

"Yeah, where you gotta be?" Johnny wanted to know.

I still wasn't telling them about the counseling. But I had to cut out of there and make it to that stupid-ass group. I had to keep that phone call from happening. As much as I hated my house, I wasn't looking for a ride to rehab.

I could do this. I could get high. I could drink. I could get a buzz and still sit through all my classes. I could pull it off. I could keep that call from happening. I could.

I walked to the counseling office without any pictures crowding up my head. No thinking about getting punched in the face, no checker games, no promises for driving lessons, no Superman capes, no beasties.

I was doing all right.

I even had a stomach full of Entenmann's chocolate chip cookies.

I was king.

I want to not feel.

Claire swiveled back and forth in her chair. "So let's take a minute to explain to Pip how group works," she said.

We were all sitting in a circle in some other counselor's

office. There was no way six people were ever going to fit in hers.

"How about you start, Paco," she said to the guy sitting next to me. He had an American flag bandanna around his head and a ponytail that hung down to the middle of his back.

"It works like this," he said. "You come here, talk about whatever, and piss in a cup before you leave. If it ever comes up dirty, you know, with any drugs or anything in it, you're screwed 'cause then Claire gets everybody in group on your ass. And 'cause nobody really wants to talk about themselves, we're cool to jump on you if you're using."

"If everybody's clean," the guy on the other side of me said, "we talk about what's going on—how we're all doing with stuff."

"Let's introduce ourselves before we get too far into everything," Claire said.

"I'm Darius," the guy who was just talking said. His head was shaved like a marine's. There was a tattoo of a dragon on his neck and he had silver rings on every finger. "I'm eighteen and I've been clean eleven months." That was hard to believe from the looks of him.

"I'm Mark," the guy next to Darius said. He was wearing overalls with the bib part hanging down on his lap. He was holding the straps in his hand and a couple of times I saw him put one in his mouth. "I been coming here a couple of weeks. How long am I clean? I don't know. Claire, was it good last week?"

"How do you *think* it was?" she asked him.

"I don't know. That's why I'm asking."

"You know if you used last week or not," she said.

"Fess up, man," said the one guy who'd been quiet up until

then. He was wearing a blue T-shirt with my brand of cigarettes and a lollipop sticking out the top of the front pocket. "If it was clean she wouldn't be bustin' on you."

He looked at me and put a hand out for me to shake. "I'm Anthony, by the way."

"So what did you find?" Mark asked her.

Claire put her elbows on her knees. "Why are we playing games? You know and I know and everybody in here knows you had a dirty urine. Now *you* tell us what you were using. This is what getting honest with yourself and others is about. It's not about you taking chances and trying not to get caught."

"Come on already," Darius said. "Stop screwing around."

"I had a joint the night before group. One joint. Big deal."

"Where'd you get it?" Anthony asked.

"I was hanging out with a guy who had some and—"

"What guy?" Anthony pushed.

"Just a guy."

"What's his name?"

I didn't know why Anthony gave a crap who it was. I figured maybe he didn't like Mark too much.

"It was Tommy, right?" Paco asked.

"Yeah. So what?"

Darius shook his head. "You hanging out with him again?"

"So it's not surprising you used that night," Claire said. "We talk about staying away from the people, places, and things that tempt you. If you put yourself at arm's length of your drug of choice, you're going to pick it up."

"He had ecstasy too, but I didn't touch that."

"You still used," Anthony said.

"You guys never slipped when you first tried to quit?" he asked.

Nobody answered.

I wasn't sure what was going on or why I had to be there for it. I wasn't like these guys. I didn't want to stop using, but if I did, I could do it whether I had stash in my pocket or not.

"This is your last slipup, Mark," Claire said. "Strike three and you're out."

"What are you talking about?" I asked.

"You get two dirty urines," Darius said. "On the third one you're out of group."

"Pip, do you want to tell us about the urine I took from you last week?" Claire asked.

"That one doesn't count," Paco said. "Right, Claire? Because he didn't start group yet."

"It counts in the bigger picture but not for getting tossed from group."

"Maybe I could get one of you guys to take care of filling my cup today," I said, smiling.

"Just don't ask Mark," Anthony said.

"You don't have to take a urine off Pip today," Mark said. He leaned against me and inhaled. "He had a couple of joints and half a brewery on the way here."

"No kidding," Darius said. "Why'd you even bother coming to group if you were going to come stoned out of your head?"

"I didn't want to come here," I said.

"Why don't you tell the guys a little bit about yourself and why you've joined the group," Claire said.

I looked at their faces. Every guy was watching me except for Mark. He was sucking on his overall strap. Claire started moving back and forth in her chair again. I didn't know what to say.

"I got blackmailed into coming here. My principal said if I didn't do the counseling gig, he was going to toss me out of school and call my house to tell the folks all about it."

"Throw you out for what?" Paco asked.

"I don't know. Stupid stuff."

"Right." Anthony laughed and shook his head.

"So what?" Mark asked. "Your principal never called your house before?"

"He never called before to tell them I was expelled and should be in a rehab."

"So what were you afraid of?" Darius asked.

"I just don't need the hassle."

"You mean you don't need your old man giving you another black eye is what you don't need," Darius said.

Who the hell did this guy think he was?

"You don't know what you're talking about," I said.

"Yeah, I do. You turned white as blow soon as I said that."

"Let's ease Pip into the group scene a little slower, Darius," Claire said. "None of you guys told your whole story in one session. Why should he?"

She put a hand on Paco's shoulder. "How about each of you share with Pip what you're doing in group and what it is that *you* want."

"We talk about that a lot in here—what we want," Paco said. "I want a girlfriend, a roll of cash, a sports car, and season tickets to the Knicks."

"But what are you really saying you want?" Claire asked.

"Love, security, mobility, and entertainment."

Anthony laughed. "Claire taught him those big words,"

"What do you want, Anthony?" Claire asked.

"A woman who makes a lot of money, who can't talk so I

don't have to listen to her bitch. She's got to cook, and I'll take one of them sports cars too."

"That's your macho answer. That's not what you've been telling me."

Anthony looked around for a second as if he was trying to decide whether he should answer. He took the lollipop out of his pocket, tore off the wrapper, and shoved it in his mouth.

"I want to be a fireman like my father and my grandfather. I can't do that if I'm drinking a keg of beer on weekends and snorting coke every day."

Mark sat up and took his strap out of his mouth. "I want to get all the assholes off my back. I got a principal too," he said to me. "I got a parole officer and a loser father and a dead mother who all get on my case in their own way."

"I want people to respect me," Darius said. "Not because they're afraid of me, or because I got the bottle to pass around or the best weed in my pocket. I want respect because I'm doing the right thing."

I laughed a little. It was all sounding like the end of some movie they show in health class.

"What's so funny?" Anthony asked. "You're so stupid, you don't even know how to use a roach clip." He looked at the group. "Check out the burn on this guy's lip."

Darius gave me a look that meant death. "You'd better not be laughing at me, punk."

"Sorry, man," I said. "You guys just sound so friggin' serious. You know, lighten up a little."

"Smoked as much weed as you did before group, we'd all be laughing too," Mark shot back.

"They sound serious because this *is* serious," Claire said.

"I figured *you'd* say that," I told her. "Don't you see these guys are just yanking your chain—saying what you want to hear?"

"Screw you," Darius said. "If you can't be serious get the hell out."

"Wish I could."

"Tell us what *you* want, Pip," Claire said.

"He don't know what he wants," Darius mumbled, looking as if he was getting ready to spit.

"I want *not* to come here, and I want everybody to get the hell off my back."

"I'm with you," Mark said.

"You just don't want your old man to kick your ass," Darius said. "That's the only reason you're here. You're scared." He smirked at me, and if I wasn't so stoned I would have decked him.

"Go to hell," I said.

"Been there and back, butthead."

"Pip," Claire said. "Think about it. It's important. What do you really want out of life?"

I want—I want—I want—I want—

Walking home from group, I was thinking about what would happen if Giraldi called the house to tell my father I was expelled and that he thought I was using drugs. I'd seriously get my ass kicked, then I'd get sent real far away to rehab. But maybe being sent away wouldn't be as bad as I thought. Maybe I could handle the biggest ass-whipping of my life and then get hauled away and never have to deal with the Grinch again.

I just had no idea what a rehab would be like. They could make you shave your head or have you running laps and doing push-ups every day. They could feed you crap like oatmeal and tofu every meal.

What I knew was a lot easier to deal with than what I didn't. I was trapped.

I couldn't go to the group stoned or have a dirty urine, or I'd get thrown out.

I had to go to the group or Giraldi was calling home.

If Giraldi called home I was dead.

I was still thinking about all this when I walked in the front door. There was a big vase on the kitchen table filled with flowers. The card was to Mom from my father. I knew without even reading it. And Mikey was playing with some super-expensive remote-controlled toy he'd been asking about for like a hundred years.

My father handed me twenty bucks as soon as he saw me.

He was feeling guilty. Maybe you could even call it feeling sorry. I'll call it being crazy. He handed me the money, then asked me what happened to my face.

No joke.

I couldn't chance having Giraldi call. I never knew what stage of crazy my father was going to be in from one day to the next.

I shook off whatever was left of the drinking and smoking I'd done that day. I shook it off and looked my life in the eye. Looked at Mikey playing as if he was some happy, normal kid. Looked at Mom on the couch with her eyes closed. At Dad, smiling at me.

When Jekyll turns to Hyde, somebody always gets hurt in my house. If Giraldi called, it would probably be me—but maybe not just me.

I couldn't take chances. Not with this. I was trapped. I needed a joint.

I remember this one time I was playing ball with my dad when I was eight years old.

"Dad?" I asked him. "Did you and Grandpa have a lot of fun when you were a kid?"

"I don't even know what fun is," he said.

Then I figured that if he didn't know what fun was, he probably wasn't having any with me either.

I had my head out my bedroom window. I was smoking a joint and a cigarette at the same time. I'd lit both, figuring if anybody walked in and caught me, I could say it was just a Marlboro they were smelling. I wasn't thinking straight.

"Whatcha doing?" Bugs asked me as he walked into my room. The kid never knocks.

I dropped the joint and let it fall out the window, but cursed when I saw it was Bugs and not the Grinch.

"Get out of here, Mikey."

"But I—"

"I said get out."

I shoved him out of my room and slammed the door behind him. I heard him stomp off into his room, then *his* door slammed.

I guess I should have let him talk. I kept pushing the kid away. But I had so much on my head already.

I went across the hall to his room and opened the door. He was sitting on the floor with action figures in his hands. They were fighting with each other. He was making pow-pow sounds and a few uggghs.

"What did you want, Bugs?" I asked him.

"Forget it," he said without looking at me.

"Come on. You wanted something."

"I beat Dad at checkers—that's all."

"That's all?"

"No." One of his action figures fell over and died. The other one stood on the dead one's chest. "I wanted to ask you something."

"So ask."

"Why does Daddy drink that stuff off the top of the refrigerator anyway?"

I rubbed my hand over my face. I didn't need this.

"Why don't you ask him?" I said.

"Forget it. I knew you didn't know."

I started to walk out of his room.

"You don't know everything—do you?" he said.

"Nobody does."

"But you know everything about you. Right?"

"I guess."

"So why do you smell like Daddy sometimes and smoke cigarettes?"

"Mikey, I'm going to bed."

"You don't know all about you either—do you?"

"Maybe I'm just not saying, Bugs."

"Daddy couldn't tell me either."

"Tell you what?"

"Doesn't matter." He got up off the floor and took his Superman pajamas out of his drawer.

I went back to my room. I took out everything I had in my

pockets and put it all on the dresser—the old bottle cap, the twenty-dollar bill, the picture of my father and me.

I wasn't worried about Bugs. He could take care of himself.

I had my own stuff to figure out.

I want to paint my walls tie-dye.

I tried. I tried not to smoke—I tried to get through the whole day of school without a joint. I had to. If I showed up at group and gave a dirty urine, I was toast. I knew Giraldi was waiting for me to screw up. He called me into his office just to ask if I was doing the right thing.

I told him to call Claire and ask her. He said he was just about to.

Go ahead. Have a friggin' party trying to screw up my life.

I couldn't sit still in school. I was ready to kill somebody. I kept taking bathroom passes just so I could get out of my seat—walk the halls. Kirkland kept me after class again to see if I was all right. If he thought I was going to tell him how I got my shiner, he was the one smoking too much weed.

Coach Fredericks threw me out of gym. I didn't want to play the stupid floor hockey game anyway. Some punk, Steven, hit me with the stick right in the friggin' shin. I wasn't my regular cool, chilled-out self, so I popped him one. Not too hard. I mean, I just shoved him into the wall and gave him a sucker punch right in the gut.

Giraldi loved it.

"I just spoke with Ms. Butler," he said. "She told me so far you're in compliance with counseling. And you've been going to all your classes too, but I can't tolerate you getting into fistfights."

"Our deal had nothing to do with that."

"Don't you think you get into enough fights, Phillip?"

"Pip."

"Look at you. Look at that shiner. You're going to go through life wearing your bad attitude on your face forever."

I just stared at him.

"You're making some changes. You're going to all your classes. But if you're going to continue to get sent to my office I won't be able to ignore that. You have to toe the line—the whole line."

He had no idea that by getting on my back, he was making it harder for me not to smoke that joint I had waiting in my sock *just in case.*

But I did it. I got through the whole friggin' school day without one toke of weed.

I picked Mikey up. Took him to T-ball practice. Read some more of that Jekyll and Hyde book, then took Mikey home.

He wanted me to shoot hoops with him outside in the driveway. Instead I smoked a cigarette and sat on the side while he took shots. He was running up and down the driveway with his Superman cape flapping over his back.

"I know why Daddy drinks those bottles on top of the fridge," he said out of nowhere.

"Why?"

"He drinks them because he's sad."

I didn't tell him how stupid I thought that was. "What makes you say that?"

"I can just tell."

"And drinking makes him so happy, he yells and chases us into the garage?"

Mikey put the ball under his arm for a second and thought about that.

"Maybe it can't make him happy," he said. "But it makes him mad and that feels better than being sad. Right?"

I flicked my cigarette across the street. I didn't know what to say.

He almost made sense.

I remember coming home from somewhere when I was twelve. I walked into the house, and my father was sitting on the couch with Mikey on his lap. The kid was like two years old. My father was smiling at him, doing googly baby noises and trying to get him to laugh.

He didn't know I was there. He was playing and then all of a sudden he stopped. His face dropped—like his head went somewhere else that made him real sad.

One second he was playing and the next he had just stopped cold.

I didn't get it.

I went to the Site for the hell of it. Where else was I going to go?

I wanted to get out of my house. I needed to get out of my house. It's just as hard to be *home* without a buzz as it is to be in school.

Johnny and Slayer weren't around—I was alone with the underground crew. I sat down against Beattie's headstone.

"Hey, man," I said to Beattie. "It looks like it's going to rain."

The clouds were doing some crazy stuff over my head. They were moving and changing faster than I'd ever seen. If I'd been stoned I'd just figure I was seeing things, but this was for real.

"I'd rather be out here in the rain," I said to Beattie. "It's better than school or home, where I can't friggin' breathe."

Then I remembered who I was talking to. "I guess I shouldn't be complaining to you. I mean, you *really* can't breathe. At least you got plenty of grass," I joked, and pulled a handful of it out of the ground.

The clouds were running a race and it was starting to get dark.

"Thanks for not asking me a lot of stupid questions," I said. "You're pretty smart for a dead guy. You know that I don't have any answers. But let me ask *you* a question."

I lit a Marlboro and blew out some smoke.

"What the hell does this mean on your pillow here? 'Beloved Husband, Loving Father.'"

The rain started falling in buckets. No drops. No sprinkles.

I lay back and closed my eyes.

The rain put out my cigarette.

I want something to do.

I got up pretty easy the next morning. I didn't have that after-high feeling from smoking the day before. It was the first time in a long while I'd gone a whole day without weed. Hell, I didn't even have a beer.

I was kind of laughing to myself. I knew I could do it. Drugs weren't my problem.

Life was.

I grabbed a Pop-Tart and drank some milk out of the carton.

Mikey was watching cartoons. Bugs (the real one) was fighting it out with Daffy Duck.

Rabbit season. Duck season. Rabbit season. Duck season.

Mom looked like hell—like she forgot to brush her hair or maybe forgot to wake up.

The Grinch didn't wake up feeling too good either.

"Mikey," he yelled. "I thought I told you no cartoons first thing in the morning."

Rabbit season.

"Sorry, Dad."

Mikey got up from the living room floor and turned off the television.

"Don't talk back," yelled the Grinch.

And the morning just went on like that. The Grinch was riding Mikey for everything. Even when I tried to jump in to get him yelling at me instead, he kept right on the little guy. Mikey was shaking from trying so hard not to cry. Eat your breakfast faster. Wash your dish. Sweep the floor. Wipe your nose. Stand up straight. When he smacked him in the back of the head, the kid finally lost it and got tears all over his shirt.

"We got to go," I said, grabbing Mikey's backpack and sort of pushing him out the door.

Walking to school, he didn't say much. He kept his head down and kicked rocks.

"How come Mom doesn't make him stop?"

I was wishing he'd just ask me something about M&M's.

"She can't do anything," I told him.

"But you do," he said. "You yell at him. You get me away from him sometimes. You—"

"I just do what I been doing since I was your age. You can do it too, you know."

He shook his head but didn't say anything until we got to the front of the school.

"Dad said last night he was still going to the zoo with me."

"Great, Bugs. You better get moving or you'll be late."

He pulled the straps on his backpack and tossed a rock into that hole before going into the building.

I wondered if he was ever going to be able to deal with stuff the way I did when I was six—the way I was still doing ten years later.

I didn't want to think about it. Thinking about how he was going to turn out when he was sixteen made me feel sick to my stomach.

I want to know what the hell I'm doing.

School sucked.

All I did was watch the red hand tick-tick its way around the clock each period. The only good thing about being there was Kirkland's class. He talked about Jekyll and Hyde and I actually had some clue of what he was saying. I got to sit next to Jenna the whole time too. She smelled like some kind of flower. I'd never really liked flowers, but whatever one was hiding out in her perfume was doing something to me.

Group made me crazy too—a bunch of guys sitting around in a circle like they were getting ready to play duck-duck-goose. I was having trouble getting used to it.

It started with Claire talking about the urine checks from the other day. Everybody's was clean except mine. Surprise, surprise.

"You clean today?" Anthony asked me.

"I took a shower," I said.

"So this guy is always going to be a wiseass then?" Darius asked.

"Did you use today?" Paco wanted to know.

"No. I didn't do anything."

Claire looked at me. "What was that like for you?" Her question was right out of some psychology book.

"It was no big thing."

Mark made some pig snort—like he wasn't buying a word I said.

"Come on," he said. "You went all day without your almighty weed and you're cool with that?"

"I could stop if I wanted to. I just don't want to."

"But now you have to," Mark said. "Or you're tossed out of high school."

"And your old man kicks your ass," Darius said, smiling.

"Lay off the old man stuff," Paco said. "The only reason *I* came here was 'cause my father dragged me by the hair. It was either this or military school."

"What's *your* old man think about you coming here?" Anthony asked me.

"He doesn't know."

"See?" Darius smiled again.

"He doesn't know shit about me. Why should I tell him about this?"

"Do you want to tell us anything about your family?" Claire asked. "Whether or not you have brothers or sisters—if your parents are divorced or together."

"My parents are still together."

I didn't want to say out loud how I wished they weren't.

These guys wouldn't be able to wrap their heads around that one.

"I have a brother too. Mikey. He's six."

That was all I was going to say. It was somebody else's turn to talk. I was tired of being on the spot.

"Does your old man hit you?" Paco asked.

I squinted my eyes into a what-the-hell's-the-matter-with-you look.

"My old man used to take a belt to me," he said. "When I got bigger he just used his fists."

"That's hard, man," I said.

"He likes to drink. He gets sauced and takes it out on me and my mama. It's better when he pops me, though. She don't take it too good."

Nobody spoke for like a minute. I sure as hell had nothing to say.

"So what happened to your eye?" Anthony asked.

"I was kissing a train—things got out of hand," I said.

Nobody said a word. Claire didn't even swivel in her chair.

"So we all going bowling tonight?" Anthony asked. "We got to keep Mark and Pip off the street."

They all started talking about hooking up at the bowling alley. *Clean and sober activity,* Claire called it. It was supposed to be one of those things to keep us away from the people, places, and things she was always talking about.

I kept quiet. They went on about where they used to hang out and the places they've been going to lately.

"You coming with us?" Darius asked me.

"No, thanks. I got something else going on."

Darius wasn't smiling. "Friday night. Of course you got something else going on. What is it?"

"Just hanging out with some friends."

"They use?" Mark asked.

"So what if they do?"

"See, Pip, they're not going to like that in here," Mark said. "You heard how they ripped into me last time."

Then they spent ten minutes trying to tell me how I should stay away from my friends. How my friends are going to bring me down and keep me using. They didn't get it. If I wanted to use I was going to do it whether I was with Johnny and Slayer or not. First Giraldi tells me I have to go to counseling, then I have to stop using, and now I have to stay away from my friends.

Screw them.

I remember playing with Matchbox cars when I was a kid. I made bridges out of blocks and ramps out of books. I made a different sound for every car. Some engines purred, some rumbled.

I was the driver for every one of them. Fire engines, tow trucks, police cars, Mustangs, BMWs, and demolition cars with the Pennzoil stickers all over them.

I was king of the road—the roads I made.

Before I went out I spent about ten minutes in my closet. I was looking at the two bags of weed Johnny had given me. The bag he gave me to smoke and the bag I was supposed to sell. I never even split that bag into smaller ones. I knew I wasn't going to sell it. I wasn't a businessman. When Johnny looked at a bag of weed, he saw a way to make money. When I looked at a bag of weed, I saw how many joints I could roll and smoke myself.

I shoved both bags back into my closet and left the house.

That wasn't easy. I'm not even 100 percent sure why I did it. Maybe because I'd already gone all day without using. I figured I'd finish out the night without the weed and keep that urine check clean.

But that didn't mean I wasn't going to drink.

I met Johnny and Slayer and a couple of other guys at the parking lot behind the post office. They had a keg of beer and everybody was smoking pot. One guy was passing around speed. I'd had two beers and was thinking about getting out of there. Standing around in a parking lot leaning against Johnny's mother's red Escort wasn't doing anything for me.

Johnny came over and put a small mirror under my chin. It was a little square mirror like the kind my mother keeps in her pocketbook.

"It's time," he said.

"What?"

"Take a hit."

I looked at the mirror and saw the two lines of white powder going across it.

"Time to take a ride on the white train," Johnny said, and handed me a rolled-up dollar bill to snort it with.

"Thanks for the cash," I said, took the dollar out of his hand, and shoved it in my jeans.

"Very funny," he said. "Come on. I saved it for you." He wiped his nose and pinched his nostrils with two fingers.

"I'm not up for this tonight."

"What's with you, man?"

I didn't want the group to be right. I didn't want to use just because I was with these guys. I wasn't about to give my friends up right along with everything else. I couldn't let go of everything.

"I'm just not into it tonight."

"You're turning out to be a real slouch. You don't hang out anymore. You go to all your classes. I know you haven't sold one speck of that weed I gave you. I want it back, by the way."

"Give me your keys," I said.

"What keys?"

"Your mother's car keys."

"What the hell for?"

I want to go.

I was at the wheel for the first time. I wasn't pushing it, though. I wasn't speeding. I didn't run any lights. I was just cruising.

But I felt free. I was doing something I've been wanting to do for the longest time. My father kept promising to take me, and here I was doing it without him. Turned out I really didn't need him at all. That felt better than being high.

"Come on," Slayer yelled from the backseat. "Floor this sucker. Let's fly."

He was *already* flying after four beers and the two lines of coke Johnny had tried to give me.

"Yeah, Pip," Johnny said. "Show us you're not turning into a total dork."

I pressed just a little harder on the gas. I didn't want to smash up the car, but I wanted to have a good time. I wanted to show the guys I still knew how to party—that I was still one of them.

My foot was heavy on the pedal for only a minute. Maybe not even a minute.

"We got company," Johnny said.

I looked in the rearview mirror and saw a cop car flashing its lights.

"Quick," Johnny said. "Switch seats with me so you don't get busted."

Johnny and I ducked down and bumped past each other in the front seat. He got behind the wheel just as the cop walked up.

"Driver's license and registration," the cop said. "Yours too," he said to me.

That wasn't the worse part. The worse part was that it wasn't just a cop. It was Officer Wanna-Be-Your-Pal from that night at the party—the one who'd brought me home.

Johnny handed him the registration from the glove box and took his license out of his wallet.

"Whose vehicle is this?"

"My mother's," Johnny said.

"Where's *your* license?" the cop asked me.

"What do you need that for?"

"You were driving the car. I want to see your license."

Johnny and I looked at each other as if the cop was crazy. We were about to say something, but he cut us off.

"Don't even waste my time, fellas. Pass the license over."

"It's home," I said.

"Let me see some I.D."

"I don't—"

"Get out of the car. All of you."

We did.

"Put your hands on the roof and wait."

I couldn't believe it. I'd been worried about getting killed for being expelled, and now it was going to end up happening because I got arrested.

The cop went to his patrol car to talk into his radio, then he came back and patted us down. The three of us kept looking at each other. We were all sweating in our own way. This was no joke.

On Johnny, the cop found three bags of weed and an envelope with enough coke for a line or two. Slayer had two joints and a couple of ecstasy pills on him.

I was clean.

Another cop showed up, cuffed Johnny and Slayer, and put both of them in the back of his patrol car. I still had my hands on the roof of Johnny's mother's car when the guys drove off.

"I remember you," Officer Wanna-Be-Your-Pal said. The name tag over his pocket said Ross. "I took you home—what was it, a week ago? And here you are again, getting into trouble on my beat just like I told you not to."

He took my hands off the roof of the car and put them behind my back.

"Like the way these bracelets feel?" he asked, tugging his cuffs on me pretty tight, then pulling me over to his car.

"No," I said. I felt as if I was going to puke.

"It's Pip, right?"

I nodded.

"Tell me something, Pip. Is this what you want to do with your life? Is this it for you—getting high, driving somebody else's car without a license, getting into fights?"

I looked away from him and stared at a Corvette speeding by.

"And look at your damn eye. Somebody got you good. Bet you had that one coming to you." He shook his head and opened the car door.

"I'm bringing you into the station house for driving without a license. I could call your friend's mother too, to find out if she ever gave you permission to drive her car. Then I could book you for car theft. I'll have to call your parents, get them out of their nice warm bed to come pick you up. Or maybe they'll let you spend the night at the precinct."

It had been my first almost totally clean and sober day. It was a day that had needed some spice to it, like being behind the wheel for the first time.

I wanted to say something, but I didn't know what. I could tell him I was trying to get it together, but he'd smell the beer on me.

"What do you have to say for yourself? Change my mind here. Say something."

Nothing made any sense to me anymore. I gave up.

"I got nothing to say. I did have this shiner coming to me. I figure I brought on getting busted too."

He pushed my head down as he put me into the patrol car.

He got in the front seat, started the car, and drove off.

I wondered what it was going to be like getting fingerprinted.

I want to not be afraid.

The cuffs were digging into my wrists. My face was getting hot and I couldn't breathe so good.

Officer Ross drove for about five minutes, then pulled over.

"I want you to tell me something," he said, turning around in his seat. "I want you to answer this question and just be honest. I want you to try that. Okay?"

"What?"

"I got into a lot of fights when I was a kid. I've seen a lot of adults kick each other's butts. But the only time I ever saw a shiner that bad was at a boxing match. That's the worst one I've ever seen." He looked out the windshield for a second, then back at me again.

"Who gave it to you?"

I blinked.

"Nobody gets into trouble because of your answer. Was it your old man?"

I was wondering why I should cover for my father. Because ever since I was a kid I learned you don't tell anybody what goes on at home? Was that a good enough reason? And who was going to cover *me*? Not my old man. I knew that much.

Ross took a stick of gum out of his pocket and shoved it in his mouth. "You don't even have to say anything," he said, while chewing. "I hear your answer just by looking at you."

He got the car going again and drove about ten more minutes, then stopped right in front of my house.

He walked past the front of the car, opened my door, and let me out. After taking the cuffs off, he put both his hands on his hips and blew some air out of his mouth.

"I'll be watching you."

I rubbed my wrists and stood in front of him. I wasn't going to move until he told me to.

"I'm wondering if you got that black eye from the last time I brought you home. Maybe you caught hell for that. I don't know." He kicked at the ground. "I might get in touch with your school and check things out there. But believe me, you don't want my cuffs on you again. You're the first second chance I ever gave, and you can count on there not being a third."

I didn't know what to say.

"No getting behind the wheel without a license—"

"I have a permit—"

"You can't get behind the wheel without a license or an adult licensed driver. Do you understand?"

"Yes."

"Go inside."

I started walking up the driveway.

"Hey," he yelled to me.

I turned around. He had a serious mean look on his face.

"Try saying thank you."

"Thanks. Thank you."

I looked up at my house. The curtain moved in Mikey's room.

I wasn't sure what was worse—the Grinch catching me being brought home by a cop, or Mikey seeing me in handcuffs.

I want to live someplace quiet.

Maybe I'll get a room next to Beattie and Agnes at the Mountain of Hope.

The house was dark. And quiet. My mouth was dry, and my head was pounding. I took some Tylenol out of the cabinet in the kitchen and opened the refrigerator to get some ice water. The light from inside the fridge lit up the kitchen. When I turned around with the pitcher of water in my hand, I saw him sitting at the table.

"Your friend Johnny's mother called—something about her son being arrested because you were driving her car."

My father was spinning his glass on the table in slow circles, sloshing his potion almost over the rim.

"That doesn't make sense. Right?" I swallowed the pills with a gulp of water. "Why would he get arrested because of me?"

"Were you driving this woman's car or is she a liar?" He drank down what was left in his glass.

"If Johnny got busted, it wasn't because he gave me his mother's keys."

"Why then?"

I wasn't going to tell him about the drugs.

"He was mouthing off, so the cop brought him in."

"Were you driving the car?"

I put my glass in the sink and started heading for the living room. It was time to get as far out of his reach as I could.

"Were you?"

"For like one minute."

He nodded his head and pushed his glass across the table.

"Get me another drink," he said.

I didn't want to. He could get his own drink. I knew that. He knew that. The whole family knew. It was all he ever did besides act crazy. He poured his drinks and he drank them.

I took the glass off the table, went over to the fridge, and took down one of the four bottles of scotch he had lined up there. I cracked some ice from the freezer and dropped the cubes into his glass. I unscrewed the bottle and poured his drink. Then I handed him his potion.

"Sit," he said.

I flopped into the seat across from him and watched him throw back his head four times to finish off the drink.

"Why'd you drive this woman's car?"

"Uh . . ." I wasn't sure what to say.

He slammed his fist on the table. "Answer me!" he screamed, his spit flying across the table at me.

We were still sitting in the dark, but I could see him. I could see his face getting red, veins popping up from his neck, his eyes getting smaller and nastier.

"Johnny was giving me a driving lesson."

"Who told you you could get behind the wheel? I never said you could drive."

"You keep saying you're going to give me a driving lesson and you keep not doing it."

"Just like I kept telling you to clean the garage and *you* kept not doing it."

This was going to get out of hand, and the last thing I needed was another black eye. I stood up and was about to say I was going to bed, when he jumped up out of his seat.

"Let's go," he said.

"Go where?"

"You want a driving lesson. You're getting one now." He grabbed his keys from off the kitchen counter and went out the door. "Let's go!" he yelled.

I wanted to slam the door behind him and lock him out like I'd locked him out of the garage. It just wasn't going to work the same way this time. He'd huff and puff and blow the house down. Then he'd beat my face in.

■ ■ ■

I remember one day when I was eleven. I was sitting in the backseat of the car and Mikey was next to me in his car seat.

Dad was driving. Mom was going through her purse looking for something.

He started screaming at her that she loses everything. She yelled back that he was going to scare the baby. He took his hands off the wheel while the car was still going, and told her to drive if she was going to be such a bossy bitch.

She grabbed the wheel and the car went to the left.

He pushed her hands away and got the car going straight again.

"See what I mean about you?" he said.

Then we got where we were going. For ice cream.

"So put it in reverse," he yelled at me as soon as we got into the car.

"Let me get the key in the ignition first."

I turned the key and got set to shift.

"What's the matter? You afraid now? Tough guy on the road with your friends and now you're a wimp?"

"What are you talking about?"

"Shut your yap and let's get on with this."

I yanked the gearshift down as hard as I could. I floored the gas with my right foot and put my left foot down just a little on the brake. The car screeched so loud down the driveway, it probably woke up the whole block.

"Stop!" he yelled.

I slammed on the brake at the bottom of the driveway.

What would it be like, I wondered, to floor the gas and send us both flying into a tree?

"Get out," he growled. "You don't know how to drive. You're an irresponsible, good-for-nothing wiseass."

I put the car in park, took the keys out of the ignition, and opened my car door.

"You've got no business on the road."

"You've got no business with a family," I said, not caring if he heard me.

I left the door open and started walking up the driveway. He jumped out of the car and walked real fast after me.

"You think you're better than me?" he asked, turning me around and putting his face not even an inch away from mine.

I stuck my chin out and waited.

"You think all the screwing around you do is something you're going to grow out of? I got news for you—this is who you are and this is who you'll always be."

He shoved my chest and I tripped back a step, then got right in front of him again.

"You get yourself in the house now, mister."

I shoved the keys at him. "Thanks for the driving lesson," I said, and walked away.

"Forget about any driving lessons until you're eighteen," he yelled.

"Go to hell," I said real low.

"And you're grounded for two weeks."

That's hell.

I want some more good stuff to remember.
The kind you put in a picture album and like looking at.

■ ■ ■

The door slammed downstairs. I was in the bathroom, sitting on the edge of the tub, waiting.

I was waiting to see if he was going to go to bed or come at me to finish things off.

I wanted to light up a cigarette, but figured I'd really be pushing it if I got caught smoking in the house. My hands were shaking. I could still feel the metal from the cuffs digging into my wrists. The pictures in my head were flashing nonstop. Dad at the table, Mikey eating my pot, Darius giving me crap in group, Johnny holding the mirror under my nose.

I didn't really want a cigarette. I wanted a joint. I needed a joint.

The Grinch didn't come upstairs. I heard him and Mom yelling at each other. He was telling her what a go-nowhere loser I was. She was telling him to keep his voice down. I didn't hear him say anything about a cop bringing me home, so he either didn't see or he'd forgotten already.

They were yelling back and forth, but it sounded as if the old man was winding down. He wasn't headed for one of those really big blowouts. So I unlocked the bathroom door and went into the hall.

Mikey's bedroom door was closed. I opened it a little and looked in to see if he was asleep.

He wasn't in his bed.

I looked around the room and didn't see him. I put my hand on the mattress—it wasn't warm. The stuffed Bugs Bunny I got him a couple of Christmases ago was on his pillow.

"Mikey?" I started moving stuff around his room, checking to see if he was hiding. Then I went into my room to see if he was camped out there. He wasn't.

I went crazy calling his name, looking around my room,

then back in his, under his bed, behind his desk. Then finally in his closet.

He was sitting on the floor with his chin and his knees in his chest. I thought he was asleep.

"Bugs?"

He picked up his head, and I could see he was wearing his Superman cape and holding something. That second I knew it was going to be one of those pictures in my head that wasn't ever going to go away.

He was holding a bottle—one of my father's. He had it under his arm as if it was a teddy bear.

"I couldn't do it, Pip."

I was stuck where I was standing. I couldn't get myself to him or get my eyes off him.

"Do what?"

"I couldn't open it," he said. "I kept trying and trying." He put the bottle out for me to take. "Can you do it?"

I took the bottle out of his hand. I wanted to smash it, but I didn't have the guts.

FOUR

I remember when I was a kid and all the other kids at school would get psyched when it was Friday. They couldn't wait to have two days off of school.

All I could think of was how that meant two days at home with my father.

Friday was the day of the week I walked home the slowest.

It wasn't easy being home all weekend. My father gave me a hundred things to do around the house. I cleaned out two closets, organized the kitchen cabinets, and wiped down all the windows—inside and out.

It was a long weekend.

I couldn't even get out of the house to grab a slice of pizza. And there was no way I was getting down the block to sneak a joint either, but I thought about it—a hundred times.

This was the first time since I was a kid that I couldn't wait for Monday to come. I'd go anywhere to get out of that house—even school.

So by the time I got to first period on Monday, I was ready. I was ready to get through every class. I just wished that one of my classes was about how to smoke a joint and still come up with a clean urine.

Johnny would know—I just had to find him. I'd called his apartment a couple of times on the weekend, but his mother always answered, so I hung up. I didn't want her hassling me about driving her car. But I figured Johnny would know how to get around the urine thing. I just had to come up with a reason why I wanted to know, without telling him I was in counseling.

I looked all over school and I couldn't find him or Slayer.

"Hey. Heard your buddies got busted," one of the jocks from the party said while giving me a shove on his way down the hall.

"Yeah. They got in trouble for picking up a prostitute," I said. "How *is* your mother, anyway?"

I ducked out of the way of his swing, then he stepped off because Giraldi was coming down the hall.

"How come wherever there's trouble, you're always right in the middle of it?" he asked me.

"Why are you always following me around?" I answered.

He folded his arms across his chest. "How are you handling the news about your friends? I got a call from the youth officer about Frank and John. They're in a world of trouble, those two."

"They're not in school?"

"They're going in front of a judge today. Possession of nar-
cotics with the intent to sell. And your friend John already had
a run-in six months ago for possession of marijuana."

"So what are you going to do? Expel them?"

"Frank may be right behind you with the counseling,
depending on what his soon-to-be probation officer suggests.
John may be looking at doing time."

The bell rang and the halls emptied out. It was just me and
Giraldi.

"I'm late," I said.

"I'll walk you to class."

We headed down the hall.

"That could be you in front of the judge this morning,
Phillip. That would make things a hell of a lot worse for you at
home than being expelled."

I thought about it. If he hadn't sent me to counseling I
wouldn't have cared whether or not I had drugs in my urine. I
would have been wasted out of my head when the cop pulled
us over, and he would have found stash on me too.

But I wasn't feeling any kind of thank-you coming out of
me.

We stopped in front of my classroom. I could see Jenna in
the front watching Kirkland. She looked so fine. So right. So
everything a girl who'd never bother with a punk like me
would be.

"Apparently I'm not alone in keeping a close eye on you,"
Giraldi said. "Officer Ross called to ask me a few questions
about you this morning."

My face got red.

"I told him you were standing at a crossroad right now, trying to decide who you wanted to be. I told him the only thing

keeping you going was the fear of getting into more trouble than you can handle. He agreed with me that fear was your best friend right now."

I wondered if they'd had tea and cookies while talking about my damn life.

He opened the classroom door and nodded to the teacher.

"Have a nice day," he said.

I didn't turn around to look at him on the way to my seat.

I want my own pizza. If I can't have the whole pie, I'll take a slice. I want my own slice just the way I like it.

"I can't take you to T-ball today," I told Mikey when I picked him up.

"I don't care," he said.

I was glad to hear it. The last thing I needed was to listen to him whine. It was hard enough to put up with when I was stoned. It would be even harder after almost four days without a joint.

"Hurry up," I told him. "I got an appointment. If I'm late I'm toast."

"Am I going to Eddie's?"

"No. Mom said since I'm grounded there's no reason to drop you off. I have to stay home with you."

"So how come we're going somewhere?"

"Shut up."

He ran to catch up with me and started tugging on my arm, smiling. "I got to show you something," he said, then stopped to open his backpack.

"We have to go, Mikey." I kept walking.

"Listen," he said, running next to me. "I got another book I can read."

I walked a little faster.

"Come on, Mikey. Hurry up."

"Run, run, run. I run." He turned the page. "Play, play, play. I run to play."

"Let's get moving, Mikey."

"Fall, fall, fall. I fall down."

He turned the page again and I started walking even faster.

He ran to catch up and was reading even louder.

"Cry, cry, cry. I fall and cry."

"Move, move, move," I said. "I kick your ass."

"*Pip.*" He was starting to whine.

"Put your damn book away," I told him. "I don't have time for this crap."

He closed the book and mumbled, "You're just like Dad." I stopped walking and turned right around to look at him. "What did you say?"

"Nothin'."

"No. What did you say?"

He shoved his book in his backpack, zipped it up, and walked away from me.

"Answer me," I said, turning him around.

"I thought you didn't have time for this crap."

He pulled away from me and kept walking.

He was right. I didn't have any time.

I remember my father taking me to the library when I was five years old.

"You can write your name, can't you?" he asked me.

"Sure I can."

"Write it here," he said, pushing a paper my way.

P-I-P, I wrote.

A few minutes later I had my own library card.

"Congratulations," my father said. "Make sure you wear it out— put a lot of miles on it."

We picked out a ton of books to bring home and he read every one of them to me.

Who was that guy?

"So that's your little brother?" Claire asked me.

"More like my son," I said, thinking that would be the end of it. But she was all over that like green on weed.

"You take care of him a lot?"

"I walk him to school and pick him up after."

"That's a big responsibility."

"Somebody's got to do it."

"Why can't one of your parents?"

"Good question."

I looked around her office to see if there was anything new.

"Still didn't get a clock, did you?"

"Why do you think I need a clock?"

"I already told you. So I'll know how many more minutes I have to be here."

"If you're the one who needs to know, you should be the one to get the clock."

"You told me that already."

She started doing that swiveling thing in her chair. Lucky for her I don't get motion sick.

"So how have you been liking the group?"

"It's stupid, but I got to do it. Right?"

"You don't have to do anything you don't want to do. You have choices."

"Yeah. Right."

"It looks like you made the choice not to get high. Your last urine was clean, and you don't look stoned right now."

"Not really my choice either."

"If I wasn't doing the urine checks you'd be getting high?"

"Got that right."

"What has it been like for you to be clean?"

"Like I live in a foreign country, can't speak the language, hate the food, and everybody looks funny. It sucks."

"It won't always feel that way."

"I know," I said, figuring that someday I was going to find a way around her urine tests.

I want to make up my own mind without anybody else talkin' at me.

Claire wasn't letting anything go. "So you said the other night that you were hanging out with some friends that use."

"Yeah."

"Was it hard for you to stay clean?"

"No, I had a couple of beers. That helped."

"Well, thanks for your honesty."

"Why shouldn't I tell you I had a couple of beers?"

"You should be abstaining from all mood-altering substances—drugs *and* alcohol."

"Being here alters my mood. Maybe I shouldn't come."

"How has it altered your mood? What are you feeling?"

"I'm pissed. I want to get out of here."

"What are you pissed about?"

"This whole thing. I have to come here. I have to go to all my classes. I can't get high. You don't think I should hang out with my friends. And now you're telling me I can't have a couple of beers. Why don't you just cut my friggin' arms off while you're at it?"

"Things are changing pretty fast. It can get easier, though, once you let go."

"Let go of what? What the hell are you talking about now?"

She stopped moving around in the chair and leaned in. "You keep a lot inside you, Pip. I don't think anybody knows who you really are. The guys in group keep asking, but all you do is come back at them with smart remarks. When you stop feeling the need to go through life all on your own, you'll see that things are going to get a lot easier for you."

She was starting to sound like a bumper sticker.

"I'm not on my own. I have my friends."

"Do they know you? The ones who use—do you tell them about you?"

I was going to say yes because I always figured nobody knew me like Johnny and Slayer. But then I thought about how I'd never told those guys about the counseling. So what? We didn't have to tell each other about every little fart to know we were still tight.

"Trust me. You'll feel a lot better when you stop keeping everything bottled up inside of you."

Bottled up.

There you go.

■ ■ ■

I remember when I believed what people told me.
I don't remember what you call that.

"Let's go, Bugs," I said to him. My session was over. I'd pissed in the cup and I could finally get out of there.

He shoved his book in his backpack and wiped some potato chip crumbs off his face.

"We going home?" he asked.

"Yeah. Why?"

"I want to go to the store."

"What for?"

"M&M's."

"No way."

I opened the door and walked outside. He was right behind me.

"Pip? Know what?"

"What?"

"I'm going to the zoo tomorrow. My teacher said we're going to see monkeys and dolphins and elephants and leopards and bats."

"Bats?"

"That's what she told us."

"Dad still going with you?"

"He said to stop asking him but he's coming."

We kept walking. I lit a cigarette. Bugs popped a wad of bubble gum in his mouth.

"Pip?"

"What now?"

"Who was that lady you had to see?"

"Doesn't matter. Just somebody I'm supposed to talk to."

"Why?"

"I don't know. Now shut up."

He couldn't do it. "Pip?"

"What?"

"Is she going to fix you?"

Great. My brother thought I was broken.

I want something nobody can give me—something nobody can get. What the hell is it?

Mom was home when we got there.

"What's she doing on the couch?" I said out loud, not thinking Mikey was going to answer me.

"She always is. Soon as she gets home, she closes her eyes."

I didn't know about that. I stayed out of the house as much as I could, but Mikey had to be there. He couldn't just run to the store. He didn't have a place like the Site to go to. It was as if he was always grounded, I guess.

"Mom?" I went over to her. She had her head on a couch pillow and was curled up with her legs to her chest and her arms over her face.

"She's not going to answer you," Mikey said. "She has to rest."

Mikey was real used to this. I could tell. He was used to a mother who slept, a father who screamed, and a brother who liked to disappear and was always telling him to shut up.

I looked in my pockets to see how much cash I had on me. I found five dollars and that stupid old bottle cap. I just kept carrying it around, and I didn't know why.

"Mikey, watch some TV or something. I'll order a pizza."

Mom didn't budge when he turned the TV on.

Five dollars wasn't going to cover the pie. I went into the kitchen to grab a ten from Mom's pocketbook. I zipped it open, took out the wallet, and pulled out a ten. When I shoved the wallet back in, something rattled.

It was a bottle.

A pill bottle.

I opened it. She had seven left and the label said there'd been thirty in there to start with.

Valium.

No wonder she was sleeping so much. From the date on the bottle, she had to be taking one or two of them a day.

My father had his bottles lined up on the fridge. I never would have guessed my mother had her own stuffed in her purse.

I had even caught Mikey hanging on to one like it was a friggin' teddy bear.

Maybe Claire was onto something.

Maybe my whole family was bottled up.

I remember having this nightmare all the time when I was a kid. I'd be dreaming that my parents were screaming real loud and stuff was getting thrown around. Then some super loud crash in the dream would wake me.

I'd sit up in bed, look at my alarm clock, and tell myself it was just a dream.

Then I'd hear a crash downstairs and someone would yell.
My parents could find a way into my head even when I was asleep.
It was always hard to close my eyes again after that.

The pizza box was empty, and Mom was putting dishes in the sink and wiping off the table. She looked as if she was moving in slow motion. She'd probably been acting like this for months, but I'd never seen it before. I wasn't used to walking around my house without something between me and the rest of the world. Seeing that my mother had the same problem made it even harder.

Mikey was in the hall with my old bottle cap collection, playing some game like marbles. He was flicking the caps into the wall and bouncing them off each other. The Grinch was sitting in front of the TV, watching the news with a glass in one hand and the remote in the other.

I couldn't leave the house, so I figured I'd go up to my room and finish that Jekyll and Hyde book. Kirkland was giving a quiz, and what the hell—if I was going to have to be there I may as well know some of the answers. Jenna might think that was cool.

I read for a while—not something anybody'd ever catch me doing. But the book wasn't that bad.

There was a crash downstairs. I waited a sec, then heard my father screaming his head off. It sounded as if he was going after Mikey.

I ran downstairs. Everybody was in the kitchen. Mom was trying to hold Dad back, and Mikey was on his knees on top of the refrigerator.

The kitchen floor was covered with scotch and broken glass.

Mikey was crying and shaking on top of the fridge. "I'm sorry," he said with snot dripping off his nose.

"I'm going to bust *you* now," Hyde yelled at him. "Get down from there."

"What happened?" I asked.

"It was an accident," my mother said.

"Accident?" Hyde pushed past her and crunched his shoes right into the mess to get closer to Mikey. "What the hell were you doing up there?"

"I said I'm sorry."

Mikey was crying so hard, you couldn't even see his eyes, and his nose was dripping into his mouth. He was looking real scared but he wasn't stupid. When Hyde put his hand up to pull Mikey down, the kid leaned back against the wall.

I pushed in front of my father. "Leave him alone," I said. I figured if he came after me it would give Mikey a chance to get away.

"Back off," he yelled. He pushed me so hard, I fell on the floor, slamming my hands into the mess. I pulled a slice of glass out of my left palm. Both hands were stinging.

Hyde grabbed Mikey down off the fridge and smacked him in the head. He screamed at him, then smacked him again across the cheek. I jumped up and, with everything I had in me, smashed my body into his. He swung at me and I ducked, then pushed Mikey over to where Mom was standing. She threw her arms around his chest and held him tight.

Hyde took another poke at me and got me right on the chin.

I wanted to hit him back. I wanted to have it all out with him right there. I could have probably done some damage too, because he was sauced and I was clean. I had the energy, the clear head, and the anger all on my side.

But Mikey needed me. The longer he stayed in Hyde's sight, the more chance there was that he'd get creamed. He was the one who'd knocked over the bottles.

I shoved my father back, giving myself just enough of a head start to pick Mikey up and carry him out the door. Hyde wasn't going to chase us outside the house—not in front of the neighbors.

My father was yelling something, but all I could hear was the same old growl. I didn't care. I just ran.

I ran and I ran. Like Mikey's book that he tried reading to me—ran, ran, ran.

Then when we got about a block away, I tripped on my shoelaces and we fell on the concrete. Mikey scraped his cheek and I landed on my hands and elbows. I could feel the dirt go right up into the cuts in my palms.

Mikey was crying real hard.

Cry, cry, cry. I fall and cry.

Some part of me felt like doing it too.

I just couldn't remember how.

I want to know when the hell all this started.

We went back about an hour later. The Grinch wasn't there.

Mom said he'd gone to the store. Of course he had—he probably couldn't wait to replace the bottles that broke.

"Are you all right?" she asked Mikey.

I figured he was going to run over to her, let her hug him and give him cookies or something.

But he just said he was okay, and then went right upstairs.

I was thinking he was going to his room to play with his action figures or to practice his reading. But when I went up to check on him, he was sitting on my bed with his pillow.

"Can I sleep with you tonight?"

"I don't know, Bugs, I—"

"Please," he said. "I'm afraid of the beasties."

"Beasties, huh?"

He nodded.

There was no such thing as beasties, but there *was* such a thing as Dad, so I let him stay.

"Hey, Bugs. What were you doing up there anyway—on top of the fridge?"

"I was trying to get a bottle but it fell."

"Why'd you want one of the bottles?"

"I just wanted to see."

"See what?"

"I just wanted to see, that's all."

I watched him for a second, then I asked, "So, did you? Did you see?"

He didn't answer me.

I let it go.

Things stayed quiet all night. Nobody ever came upstairs. I guess Mom crashed early, and Dad probably had some drinking to catch up on.

When I opened my eyes in the morning, Mikey was standing next to the bed by my head. He had his Superman cape on and Bugs Bunny under his arm.

"Knock-knock," he said.

"Get lost," I told him, and put my pillow over my head.

He picked up one end of my pillow and talked under it. "Knock-knock."

"Whoever's there, go away."

"It's Barbie."

"Barbie who?" I figured I'd better play along or he'd never leave.

"Barbie-Q-Chicken."

He laughed his head off, and I pulled the pillow tighter on my ears.

"Great, Bugs, now go downstairs and have breakfast."

"Knock-knock."

"Who the hell's there now?"

"Don."

"Don who?"

"Don just lie there. It's time to get up."

He pulled the blanket off of me and ran out of the room.

Butthead.

He forgets pretty fast sometimes how scared he is. It's like he wakes up every day trying to play the family game of let's-pretend-nothing-happened. He tries to play it, but by the time we're halfway to school he still ends up shooting a million questions at me. I'd have to help him grow out of that. Teach him the rules: Say nothing. Expect nothing. Ask nothing, and nobody lies to you.

I took a quick shower, got my coolest purple-and-blue tie-dyed T-shirt on. I grabbed five dollars off my dresser and shoved it into my pocket with the bottle cap. This bottle cap thing was getting to be a habit. At school I kept pulling it out of my pocket and tossing it as if I was playing heads-or-tails. Sometimes I'd just stick my hand in my pocket and rub my thumb around the edge.

Down in the kitchen I figured everybody would be playing

the pretend game. Nobody would say anything about what happened with Mikey and the bottle. Mom would be cooking some big breakfast and Dad would be whistling and reading the paper.

I was wrong.

Mikey was sitting at the table stomping his feet and crying about how it wasn't fair.

"You just watch your mouth," my father was saying.

"Then *you* do it," Mikey said to Mom.

"I can't. I have to work," she said.

"This sucks," he yelled.

"You're lucky I'm letting *you* go," the Grinch said. "But I'm not taking time off work to reward you for the crap you pulled last night."

"What's going on?" I asked.

"Oh look," my father said. "Here's Superman now. Maybe *he'll* bail you out." He grabbed his keys and briefcase, and walked out of the house.

"Don't ever come back!" Mikey screamed. "I hate you!"

I couldn't believe it. I'd never seen him like this before. Bugs was buggin' out.

"Stop that," my mother said. "Finish your breakfast."

"No. And I'm not going to school."

"What's going on?" I asked again.

"You were right," Bugs said. "He wasn't ever going to go to the zoo with me."

Mom picked up her purse and looked inside, probably to check how many pills she had left. She took a twenty-dollar bill out and put it on the table for him.

"Get yourself a souvenir," she said, and started playing with his hair. "You'll have a better time without your father anyway. Trust me. He's no fun at these things."

"I hate him," Mikey said.

"No you don't," she said. She kissed the top of his head. "You're just disappointed."

"How do you know?" I asked her. "Maybe he does hate him."

Mikey didn't look up. He was staring into his bowl of soggy frosted flakes.

"I'm late for work," she said to me. "You need to get your brother to school."

She smiled at Mikey, but he didn't look at her.

"Enjoy your trip," she said. "You'll be fine."

Then she left.

Mikey had this look on his face I'd never seen before. He was trying to be real angry. Trying to push the sadness way down into his belly where he wouldn't feel it.

"We better go," I said.

"I'm not going on the stupid trip." He had his arms across his chest.

"What are you acting so surprised about? I told you he wasn't going to go to the zoo with you."

"So what? You don't know everything."

"Stop being a baby."

I grabbed him by the shoulder of his shirt and got him to the door. "Move it," I said. "I got to get to school too."

All I needed was Giraldi on my case for being late.

Mikey went out the door without his lunch or his backpack. I grabbed them both, then took the money my mother had left on the table and shoved it into my pocket. There was no way Mikey was going to buy a souvenir, but I could do a lot with twenty bucks.

■ ■ ■

I want a day off—from everything.

"You got to be tough," I told him on the way to school. "You can't let this stuff get to you."

He didn't answer me. It was the first time he'd ever gone the whole way to school without talking. He didn't say a word. He didn't ask me a single question.

All the kids in the first grade were piling onto the buses when we got to the parking lot. Mikey's teacher yelled for him to hurry because they had to leave.

"Where's your father?" she asked.

Mikey walked past her and got on the bus.

"He got sick," I told her.

"I'm sorry to hear that. Is your brother feeling okay? He doesn't look well."

"He's just bummed about our father."

I looked up at the bus and saw Mikey getting into a seat by the window right next to where I was standing.

"Thanks for getting him here," she said. She got on the bus and the driver pulled the door shut.

I slapped my hand on the window where Mikey was sitting, but he didn't turn his head to look at me.

The other kids were all squealing and laughing, and then they started singing.

Ninety-nine bottles of beer on the wall, ninety-nine bottles of beer.

Mikey wasn't singing. Hell, I wouldn't sing that stupid song either.

He finally turned his head and looked right at me.

We knew what that song was about.

We knew the deal—

If one of those bottles should happen to fall . . .

I remember the first time my baby brother walked. He had his hands on the coffee table and his feet were bare.

I had something he wanted. I don't remember what it was, but he wanted it. So he let out a yell like Tarzan or something, and took three steps right over to me. He laughed, then fell over into me like a tree that got cut down.

"You're in no position to come to school late."

Giraldi was sitting behind his desk looking at me as if I'd just robbed a bank. "You have detention today," he said.

"I can't do it," I told him. "I have to get my brother from school."

"You'll have to make other arrangements."

"This is messed up," I said. "You keep talking about being responsible, but it's okay for me not to get my brother from school when I'm supposed to."

He tapped his pen on the desk. "There isn't anybody else who could get him?"

"Like who?"

Giraldi didn't answer me.

"I want you to see Ms. Butler today—get a urine test."

"What the hell for?"

"I want to make sure you weren't cutting school this morning to get high."

"This is such crap."

"You won't tell me why you were late, just that something came up. That's not a good enough reason. Since you can't do detention, then you find a way to see the counselor."

Then Giraldi the control freak dialed her number with me sitting there, and made me get on the phone to set up a time with her for after I picked up Mikey.

I wanted to jump out of myself. I felt as if I had this extra layer of skin that I needed to shake off. I wanted a joint so bad. No, not just a joint—a whole bag of weed. I had plenty waiting for me at home but I had a urine check waiting for me too. I had to find a way around all this. There had to be a way.

Without a buzz, I didn't feel like me. A clean me wasn't the real me.

I didn't *want* it to be either.

I want to not want.

"How was the zoo?" I asked Mikey on the way home from school.

"Stupid," he said, not looking at me.

"You hungry?"

He shrugged his shoulders.

"I got to go talk to that lady again today, so I figured we'd grab a couple slices of pizza on the way."

"Whatever."

He wasn't talking. He wasn't goofing around. No knock-knock jokes. No questions. Not a word about M&M's. Something was up with the kid. I was hoping some soda and pizza would set it right.

157

We ate the slices while we walked, but he still had nothing to say. After a few minutes I stopped thinking about it. It was kind of a break for me not having to listen to him yap for a change.

I want all the questions to stop.
I want more answers.

We sat on the couch in the waiting room. My cigarette pack was digging into my front pocket, so I pulled the box out and put it next to me. I had a book of matches in the plastic around the pack, and I slid it in and out while I waited. There was nothing else to do. Mikey was picking at his fingernails. Claire was taking her time getting out there to me.

Between seeing her twice and the two group sessions coming up, I was going to have been in that damn office four times in one week.

"Hello," Claire said, coming down the hall.

I got up to go to her office but she stopped in front of Mikey. She put a hand out for him to shake and he sort of took it.

"My name is Claire," she said. "You're Pip's brother?"

"I'm Mikey," he said.

"Nice to meet you, Mikey. Do you have something to do while you're out here waiting for your brother?"

"I have to read a book."

I took *Jekyll and Hyde* out of my back pocket and threw it on his lap. "Try this one," I said.

I was done with it. I'd read the whole thing and taken the quiz. He could have it.

"He's got your eyes," Claire said when we got into her office.

"No, he doesn't. His are blue."

"He's got your look."

"What look?"

"That look that says back off."

"Mikey? He's like the friendliest kid in the world. He'd follow anybody home if they had a bag of M&M's."

"Hm." She started swiveling in her chair. "I don't see it. He looks—I don't know—angry, I guess is the right word."

"He's having a bad day."

"Is that it?" She let her eyebrows go up. "I don't think one day teaches you how to have eyes like that."

"What are you talking about?"

"Never mind. Tell me why we're having an extra pow-wow today."

"Giraldi has nothing better to do than bust my chops."

"What happened?"

"Why should I tell you? So you can call him and let him know you got it out of me?"

"You know I can't tell him what you say in here."

"So why'd he say he wanted me to come here for a urine check? To hear from you whether or not it's clean, right?"

"Come on, Pip. A dirty urine wouldn't prove anything anyway. That could mean you got high last night, not necessarily this morning."

"Give me a cup anyway."

"I'm not taking urine from you today. I'm more interested in knowing what happened this morning. Whatever it is had to be pretty damn important for you to risk blowing things for yourself at school."

Did she really think I'd ever give up the whole story—that

I'd ever tell her anything about me or my family? She had me confused with those punks in group.

"My brother was screwing around and got us both late. That's all."

She sort of looked me over for a second. "What happened to your hands?"

For a second I didn't know what she was talking about. Then it hit me—the Grinch pushing me down into the glass in the kitchen, falling down in the street with Bugs. Even when I took a shower that morning I hadn't been thinking about my hands until the soap stung like a son of a bitch.

Then I forgot all about it again.

It's not like how Mikey pretends nothing ever happens. What I do is stuff it in my head with all the other pictures. The counseling thing was like having somebody trying to pull the pictures out of my head—forcing me to look at them. Who the hell needs that?

"How did your hands get all cut up like that?"

"I fell."

"It must have been a nasty fall."

I didn't say anything. I didn't have to.

"Pip. How come after seeing you, what is it now, four times, five times? How come I don't feel like I know you any better?"

"Hey, I don't piss in a cup for just anybody."

"You don't say much about yourself. You don't give a lot of details and you never talk about your family."

"Why do you want to know about them?"

"It's not *them* I want to know about—it's you. Who do you go home to when you leave here? Do you like them? What's it like where you live? How do you get along with your brother and how'd you get the job of taking care of him so much?"

The pictures were speeding through my head—crazy stuff like the pill bottle in Mom's pocketbook, her sleeping on the couch, getting my first driving lesson from my father, Mikey on top of the refrigerator, me in handcuffs.

"I never said much about *my* family when I was growing up either," Claire said.

"You had to go to counseling?"

"No. But if anybody asked—even my girlfriends—I wouldn't answer. And I never let anybody come to my house."

"Why not?"

"My two sisters, my mother, and I lived with my grandparents. My grandfather was a big boozer. He drank every day but Sunday. Whiskey, rum, wine, anything he could get. He was sloppy, he smelled, he sang the dumbest songs, and sometimes, you never knew when, he got real mean."

She looked up at the ceiling for a second as if she was seeing it all in her head.

"At the end of the week he put on his Sunday best and served as the church usher, smiling at everybody like he was the most regular guy in town."

"Nobody knew he was a drunk?"

"It was our secret. My family always said what happened in our house stayed in our house. It wasn't anybody else's business."

I knew that rule.

"Did you want to tell your friends about your grandfather?" I asked.

"I wanted to tell somebody. The crazy thing is you'd think my sisters and I would have talked to each other. We didn't. One of us would get a slap in the face and no one would say a word about it."

"Why?"

"Somewhere along the way we all learned that it wasn't all right to talk about certain things. After working through my own stuff, letting out all the secrets and becoming a counselor, I realized that the reason we didn't talk about it was because we were ashamed. We even thought in some way that maybe it was our fault—that we should have been able to stop his drinking."

"How?"

"If we were prettier or smarter, kept the house cleaner, or got better grades."

"That doesn't make sense."

"A lot of things don't make sense in an alcoholic family."

I looked at my palms for a second. They were red and sore. I wanted to say something but I didn't know what.

"Your face just changed when I said that. What were you thinking?"

"Nothing," I said.

But she could have been right. Maybe my face did change a little. Something hit me when she said that word.

Alcoholic.

I remember playing outside with a friend who lived across the street. We were shooting hoops in his driveway, goofing around. His father came out and made a few shots. Then out of nowhere he put his arm on my shoulder and asked me if everything was okay.

"Sure. Why?" I asked him.

"I just heard things getting a little loud in your house last night and—"

"I heard it too. It came from down the block," I said. "It wasn't my house."

■ ■ ■

"Do you smell something burning?" Claire asked me on our way into the waiting room. She took a big sniff and looked around the place.

I smelled it. But I didn't have to look around. All I had to do was look at Mikey. He had my pack of cigarettes and was trying to light up. He couldn't do it right, though, because he didn't know he was supposed to inhale.

"What are you doing?" I asked him, grabbing the cigarette out of his mouth.

"Nothing."

I took the matches out of his hand and stuffed the pack of cigarettes into my front pocket. "I told you to stop touching my stuff."

I grabbed his sleeve and pulled him up. Hard. "What's the matter with you? You stupid or something?" I yanked on his shirt. I was ready to let him have it. Six years old and he's trying to light up a cigarette! He could have started a fire or burned himself.

"Pip." Claire put her hand on mine to get me to let go. "Take it easy," she said.

My face was hot. I was breathing hard and I felt as if I wanted to smash him.

"He keeps doing crazy shit like this," I said, and took a step back from him.

Mikey pulled his shirt where I grabbed it and looked as if he was trying not to cry.

"Let's go into my office and talk about this," she said, and put her hand on Mikey's back to get him down the hall.

I stood in the waiting room for a second. I didn't want to go back in there. I didn't want to talk to her anymore. Everything had gotten worse since I'd started going to counseling. Nothing was better. I was done talking, and she thought I'd never even started.

But I had to follow them. It was one of those choices I didn't have.

In Claire's office Mikey flopped into my chair and she nudged me to sit in the one across from him. She got in her desk chair and let out a deep breath.

"Mikey. Do you understand why your brother got so angry with you?"

He nodded his head.

"Could you tell me why you were trying to light the cigarettes?"

He shrugged his shoulders, and all I wanted to do was kill him.

"He's doing stupid stuff like this all the time," I said. "The other day he's in the closet trying to open a bottle of scotch. Then for some stupid-ass reason he's on the top of the refrigerator last night. Want to know why I was late this morning? Because the baby here was throwing a little fit because his daddy wouldn't go the zoo with him."

I looked back at Mikey. "I told you he wasn't going—"

"Shut up, Pip, you stupid—"

"Don't tell me to shut up." I started to get out of my chair. "I'll pop you one right here."

"Pip," Claire said, louder than I'd heard her speak before. "Have you ever had anybody threaten to hit you, call you stupid, or yell at you like this? I don't think it makes a person feel like talking. Do you?"

I sat back in the chair and crossed my arms over my chest. I was sick of this—all of it. Mom, Dad, Mikey, Claire, Giraldi, everybody. I was going to get out of there and get higher than a kite the first chance I had.

"He's just like Daddy," Mikey said, staring at me as if *he* wanted to kill *me*.

"How's that?" Claire asked him.

"What you just said. Yelling, hitting, saying stupid."

"You think I'm like Dad?" I said. "You're saying that crap again?"

"Why does that upset you so much, Pip?" Claire asked.

I couldn't believe it. I was the one who took care of him, and I was getting put on the same page as Mr. Hyde. Screw him.

"I'm getting out of here," I said. "Walk home yourself."

"Pip, sit down." Claire sounded pissed. I wasn't sure what she'd do if I left. I didn't want her calling Giraldi, I knew that much.

I sat back down.

"Mikey, why did you try lighting the cigarettes?"

He didn't say anything. He put his head down so his chin was almost in his stomach.

"Mikey?" Claire put her hand on his leg, and he started crying.

"I'm sorry," he said.

The kid was blubbering so hard, I could hardly make out the words.

"It's okay," Claire said. "Just tell me why you did it."

He was hard to understand behind all of that crying. But I heard his answer when he got it out. He said it and then looked right up at me.

"I wanted to be like him," he said.

■ ■ ■

I want a six-pack, a bag of weed, and a few hours by myself.

Claire said she thought Mikey should be talking to some-body the way I was—or wasn't—talking to her.

I wasn't so sure.

I let up on him a little when we got out of there. I'm not sure why, but I didn't feel like killing him anymore.

I threw out the burnt cigarettes that were on the couch in the waiting room, and told Bugs to grab his backpack. I opened the door for us to leave, and almost bumped right into the last person I ever thought I'd see at a counseling office.

We stared at each other for a second, said a quick hi, and then we both just took off where we needed to go.

"Who was that?" Mikey asked when we got to the street.

I shook out the last cigarette left in my pack and lit it.

Shit.

"Just a girl from school," I said.

The last girl I wanted seeing me at a counselor's office.

I remember going to a Yankee game with my father.
Just me and him.
We ate hot dogs, he drank beer and I had a root beer. We yelled for our team, laughed, slapped each other on the back, and dropped peanuts on the ground that crunched under our feet the whole night.
I remember when I used to like baseball.

■ ■ ■

I couldn't get out of the house after we got home. Being grounded sucks.

Everything in me wanted a joint. I needed something to take the edge off so bad, just enough to catch some z's. Not that I would have been able to sleep anyway. The Grinch started screaming at around midnight.

They could fight about anything. He was yelling about some check she'd written, and she was yelling back at him about how he yells too much.

It got loud. I heard a couple of things get thrown. Mikey never came into my room. After listening to Mr. and Mrs. Crazy for a while, I went to see if the kid was all right.

He was curled up under his covers, but I could tell he wasn't sleeping. I could hear him sucking on his thumb.

"You okay?" I asked him.

I thought I saw him nod his head, but my eyes might have been playing tricks on me in the dark. His Bugs Bunny doll was by his feet with his Superman cape around its neck. I put it on his pillow.

"No thanks," he said, then pushed Bugs Bunny off the bed.

"What's with you?" I asked.

"Nothing."

I stood there for a second, trying to figure him out. He wasn't acting right—not like himself. He wasn't saying much. He didn't come in my room looking for me like he always does. He let Bugs Bunny hit the floor.

"You tell Mom and Dad about the zoo?" I asked him.

He shook his head.

"Why not?"

He shrugged.

Something crashed downstairs, and Mikey blinked hard.

"I'm going back to bed," I told him. "You want to come?"

He shook his head, and I started walking out.

"Pip?"

I stopped.

"How come Daddy didn't go to the zoo? Because of the bottles?"

"I don't know," I told him. "It's just how it is."

He didn't say anything else, so I went back to walking out of his room.

"Close my door," he said when I got to it.

I want to hear a song that really kicks. I want to get lost in it—the beat, the words, everything.

I want to get lost in something like that.

Mikey was still acting funny on the way to school the next day. He was walking a few feet in front of me, and he wasn't talking. Fine. My head was full of enough garbage without having to take on his too. I had four joints in my sock, and that was all I could think about. I had to figure out a way to get high without cutting classes and getting a dirty urine.

He started to cross the street without me, and I jogged a few feet to catch up with him.

"Wait up," I said. I grabbed the strap on his backpack to keep him on the curb.

"What do you got in here?" I asked him. The backpack was stuffed so full, the zipper looked as if it was going to bust.

"My T-ball mitt, my lunch, a sweatshirt, my cape, and show-and-tell," he said.

"What do you got for show-and-tell?"

"Man, you say *I* ask too many questions?" He shook his head—my brother the up-and-coming wiseass.

He walked into the building without tossing a rock in the hole the way he'd been doing every morning. The kid was way off.

"See you after school," I yelled, but he didn't look back. Maybe he was getting tougher. Maybe I wasn't going to have to wipe his nose for him for the rest of my life.

I ran fast. I figured if I got to the deli and Tony didn't bug me, I could get enough of a joint smoked to take a little of the edge off. This staying clean wasn't easy. It's like all of a sudden telling a baby that he can't have his bottle, or his daytime nap or his pacifier.

I sat on a milk crate, pulled a joint from my sock, and lit it. It was the longest inhale I'd ever taken. It filled my lungs and filled my head. I thought it was the smartest thing I could do for myself. Nobody knew what I needed better than me. Nobody lived in my house but my family, and nobody lived in my head but me. What did Giraldi or Claire or any of those punks in group know about what I needed to get by?

Nothing.

"Chimney Boy," Tony said as he slammed out the back door.

I took another drag as deep as I could.

"Where've you been?" he asked, putting his hand out for the joint.

"Come on, man. Let me smoke my bone. I don't have a lot of time. I'll just leave you whatever I don't finish."

"What's with you? All of a sudden you can't be late for school?"

I didn't answer him. I didn't even look at him. All I cared

about was pulling that smoke into my lungs and letting it cloud the pictures in my head.

"Life getting to you, Chimney Boy? Huh?" He shook his head. "Yeah, you got a rough life. School all day with pretty girls in tight jeans walking past your locker. Getting high with your buddies and, oh yeah, sitting next to a Dumpster while you figure out which class to cut next."

"Shut the hell up, meat cutter. Nice life *you* have. Can I have a half a pound of *stupid* sliced thin, please?"

"You're dreaming if you think you'll do any better than me. The way you're going, you'll be lucky if you get a job sweeping floors."

"What do *you* know about it?" I inhaled on the joint again and shut my eyes.

"I know you don't get anywhere in this life, not even a deli job, if you spend your spare time next to Dumpsters and in cemeteries."

He took the joint out of my hand and took two drags before throwing it on the ground.

"That's all you'll ever be if you keep going like you are, Chimney Boy. Just a punk that hangs out next to garbage and with dead people."

I nodded like he didn't know what he was talking about, and picked up my joint.

"You know what they say." He opened the back door to go inside. "You are who you hang with."

I want a girlfriend—a sweet one.
Or maybe a dog instead.

Dogs never give you crap except when you walk them.
That's what I want. A dog I'd never have to walk.

"So we've all finished *Dr. Jekyll and Mr. Hyde*," Kirkland was saying. "I'm always curious to know if a book was effective or not. Did it affect you in any way and if so, how?"

Nobody said anything. I don't think anybody knew what he was talking about.

I stared at the back of Jenna's head. I'd sat three rows behind her today. I didn't want her asking me why I was at the counseling center, and I sure didn't want her looking at my eyes and seeing I was stoned.

Kirkland let us all sit there saying nothing. He did that a lot. If we didn't answer his question, he just waited. Or sometimes he'd come out with some crazy quote.

"'It was a night of little ease to his toiling mind,'" he said this time. "'Toiling in mere darkness and besieged by questions.'"

Some girl giggled.

"Does anyone remember that quote from the book?"

More silence.

"My whole class is toiling in darkness besieged by questions." Kirkland smiled and walked in front of Jenna. "Did this book affect you?" he asked her.

"I liked it," she said.

"Did it affect you?"

"It made me think, I guess."

"Then it affected you. What did it make you think about? Anything beyond the pages of the book?"

"Secrets," she said. "We all have them. Jekyll was no different. He was embarrassed about his, I think. We all have those kinds of secrets too. It just got me thinking about that, is all."

Kirkland moved on to bother somebody else. I caught Jenna turning around to look at me. I put my eyes on the clock as if I didn't see her. I was planning to book it fast out of class when the bell rang so she couldn't stop and ask me why I was at Claire's. She already figured me to be a pothead loser. I wasn't going to turn her off even more by saying I was in counseling.

Kirkland bailed me out of talking to her. As soon as the bell rang he called me over to talk to him.

"How's it going, Pip?" He put his arms across his chest and leaned back against the radiator.

I shrugged my shoulders, hoping like hell he couldn't smell the pot on me.

"I was very impressed with your answers to the Jekyll and Hyde quiz."

A teacher had never said anything like that to me before.

"I have a feeling that book affected you." He smiled and took a piece of paper off his desk.

"Question number three," he said. "Is Jekyll good and Hyde bad? Part of your answer is 'Jekyll is like everybody else— showing one face and having another. I see people all the time saying one thing and doing something else. Girls wear makeup so nobody sees what they really look like. People smile when they want to cry, go places they don't want to go, stay places they want to leave—' "

"Mr. Kirkland, I read this already."

"Wait. The rest of your answer is very strong. 'Jekyll needs a way out. His potion lets him off the hook. He can do what he wants. He can be who he really is—a pissed off guy.' "

"Did you take points off for the curse word?"

"'If he could be Jekyll and Hyde at the same time—do and say what he really thought—he could be one person. No potion. No Hyde-ing. No good or bad.'"

I looked up at the clock. There was no chance of grabbing a couple of hits off a joint in the bathroom before my next class. "I'm going to be late," I said.

"Mr. Giraldi checked in with me this morning to ask how you're doing in class."

I rolled my eyes.

"I told him I thought you were a great student and didn't understand why he was even concerned."

"He must've fallen over when you said that."

"Now that you mention it, he almost did." Kirkland let out a little laugh. "He told me you were in some trouble and that he was keeping a close eye on you. He wanted to know what I observed in class.

"I told him I saw a young man who was struggling, but with what I didn't know. I told him you were brighter than you thought and could probably use a little guidance. He told me that was being taken care of, but he didn't say too much more about it."

I looked at the clock again.

"I didn't mention you were drinking in school last week."

I looked right at him. I don't think I blinked.

"I won't tell him you smell like pot right now either."

"What are you talking about?"

He shook his head. "I just want to invite you to think about something. From what Mr. Giraldi told me, you're taking a lot of chances. I want you to think about the book.

Think about whatever way it affected you—the way it appears in the answers to your quiz questions. Think about who you want to be. You're in control of you—nobody else is."

Who was this guy? A teacher or a preacher?

"I recently saw the Jekyll and Hyde play," he said. "There's a line in it that I loved. About how chances are something you don't take when you're lost."

The late bell rang, and I tipped my head to the door to say I had to get going.

"If you need anything—" he started to say.

"I need a late pass," I told him.

He wrote it out, and I headed for the door.

"Pip," he said when I was almost out of there. "Think about that, okay?"

"What?"

"'Chances are something you don't take when you're lost.'"

He was as bad as Claire—talking in bumper sticker language.

What did he know about it, anyway? I wasn't lost. I knew exactly where I was.

Even stupid Tony knew.

I want to find my friends.

I couldn't stop thinking about Johnny and Slayer and what had happened to them. I'd heard something about Johnny doing time and Slayer's parents sending him to rehab, but I didn't know for sure. If they were around, though, they'd show up at the Site.

I had to go there.

And I had to smoke another joint. Everything was up against me like a sharp knife cutting through my skin to the bone. I had to stop it before I bled to death. And I'd figured out a way to get around that next urine check too. I'd go in the cup just a little, enough to make it yellow, then I'd put some tap water in it. I'd water down any traces of the pot. Besides, even if it didn't work, I'd still have another dirty urine coming to me before I'd get thrown out of counseling. You get three, they said.

I ran to the Site after school and smoked all three joints left in my sock while having a long talk with Beattie and Agnes. It was just me and them now. Johnny and Slayer didn't show. I closed my eyes and told Beattie about school—about how Kirkland was trying to play counselor with me. I told him about Jenna still looking as hot as ever, but that I couldn't talk to her.

Beattie didn't give me any advice or ask me stupid questions I couldn't answer. He just listened and didn't grub any of my pot off of me.

This was the best I'd felt in a week—maybe longer. I had nothing to worry about—nobody to think about but me.

Then I remembered Mikey.

I forgot to pick him up from school.

I want to go to the M&M's factory so I can get the answers to all the really important questions.

You can't run very fast after a few joints—you just can't. But I moved pretty quick.

My mind was going even quicker, worrying that he wouldn't still be there when I got to the school. I knew he was too smart to go off with a stranger or anything like that, but what if he just took off by himself? What if I couldn't find him?

I almost got hit by a Buick as I tore ass across the street to the school. I didn't see Mikey anywhere, but I did see an ambulance pulling out of the parking lot. Two cops were talking to each other by a patrol car.

I looked around for Bugs.

"You see a boy here?" I called to the two cops. "He's about this tall, has a Supermar backpack—"

"Like this one?" One of the cops, a tall guy with a mustache, took Mikey's pack off the hood of the patrol car he was standing next to.

"Yeah." I was out of breath. "That's it."

Both cops walked over. They were crowding me as if I had to get ready for a fight or something.

"You know the boy who belongs to this backpack?" asked the other cop, who looked like a linebacker.

"That's my brother's. You see him?"

"Yes, we saw him."

"Where is he?"

Then I thought about the ambulance I'd just seen.

"What happened to him?"

My heart was beating the hell out of my chest. My head felt like it was swelling up, and my hands were shaking.

"We've already called your mother. She's on her way to the hospital—"

"Will you tell me what the hell happened already?"

If they didn't tell me something quick I was going to start swinging.

"He was playing around over by this hole," the linebacker cop said, walking over to it. "Somebody saw him tossing bottles up in the air—one of them hit him in the head and he fell into the ditch."

I walked over to the hole and looked down. I could see the broken glass.

I could see the labels from my father's scotch bottles.

I remember the first time Mikey drank from a cup.
Big boy cup, he called it.
"No more ba-ba's," he said. So he and Mom and I took his baby bottles and threw them in the garbage. He laughed and started throwing everything in there.
A plate, a mug, a toy truck, my sneaker.

I wasn't going to stand around and talk to these guys all day. I had to get to Mikey.

I started to run off, but one of the cops caught up with me and pulled on my arm.

"Let go," I snapped, pulling it back.

"It's okay, man," the mustache cop said. "I'll give you a ride over there."

"No!" I yelled. I ran my hands through my hair for a second while I tried to think straight.

"Let us help you out," he said.

"I don't need your help," I shouted, and then took off. I ran all the way to the hospital. I *didn't* need their help. I didn't need a ride and I didn't need anybody to tell me how okay it was all going to be.

It *wasn't* okay—it was as messed up as anything could be, and it was all my fault.

I want a big brother.
One that's better at being one than I am.

While I was running to the hospital, pictures flashed in my head—Mikey throwing a rock into that hole, Mikey tossing a bottle in the air, Mikey bleeding. The ambulance taking him to the hospital, the cops looking at me, my little brother in a casket.

I found the emergency room. A nurse pointed out where Mikey was and told me I couldn't see him yet. There was a curtain around him, and all I could see were feet moving under it. Strangers were poking at my brother, and all I could do was stand on the other side of it all. All I could see were their shoes. All I could do was stand there looking stupid.

I guess I *was* stupid. I was too stupid to pick my brother up on time. I was too stupid to wear a watch.

I was biting on my thumbnail, wishing I could at least light a Marlboro.

A nurse walked by and told me to tie my shoes. "You're going to hurt yourself," she said.

Too late for that. I kept biting my nail and watching the shoes behind the curtain.

Then I heard Mikey's voice. Words weren't coming out of him, but he was trying to say something.

"Welcome back, sir," I heard a guy say.

I pushed the curtain to the side and went over to him.

"You need to wait out there," a nurse said.

"No. It's okay," the doctor guy said, smiling. I don't know what the hell he had to smile about.

"Are you a relative?" he asked. My mother wasn't there yet. Maybe that's why the doc let me in.

"I'm his brother."

I couldn't stop looking at Mikey, but he wasn't looking back. He was moving his head from side to side a little. I could tell he was really hurting. The doctor flashed a light in his eyes and felt behind his neck.

"Looks like Michael here played a little too hard today. He needs to learn to throw baseballs and footballs, not bottles. Maybe you could work on that with him. We'll keep him here a bit for observation. He seems to have suffered a concussion and has some pretty nasty lacerations to the left side of his head."

I looked at him real quick, nodded, then looked back at Mikey.

"Your parents are on their way?"

"My mother is coming."

"I'll look for her in a few then." He gave my arm a hit with the flat of his hand. "Don't look so scared. He's okay this time. We just have to make sure there isn't a *next* time. Maybe that terrific throwing arm of his could be put to better use."

He smiled again, then took off down the hall, leaving me alone with Mikey.

The kid looked so little. His feet hardly reached the middle of the gurney. His hair was all smashed down and I could see dried-up blood on his forehead and by his ear.

"Hey," I said. It was the best I could come up with. I wasn't sure what to do and I sure as hell didn't know what to say.

"You okay?" I asked.

He still had his eyes closed, but he stopped moving his head back and forth.

He said something real low. I couldn't hear him, so I put my head next to his and asked him to repeat it.

"You didn't come," he said. "I fell. You didn't come."

I should have said I was sorry.

I should have said something. Maybe I would have if my mother hadn't run in crying her eyes out.

I want to be as far away from me as I can get.

She ran right past me. Hell, she almost knocked me down getting to him. Over and over again she put her hands on his cheeks, rubbed his head, kissed him. She kept saying *poor baby, my poor baby.*

I got out of their way.

I went down the hall to the pay phone. I put a quarter in the slot and started dialing Johnny's number. Then I remembered he wasn't around.

I thought about who else I could call. Slayer was gone too. I didn't know Jenna's number, but I really didn't want to tell her about all this anyway.

The only other number I knew was Claire's from dialing it so much in Giraldi's office. It was one of those real easy numbers to remember. Still, I wasn't calling the shrink.

I hit the coin return and took my quarter back.

I checked my pocket for what I was looking for.

More change.

■ ■ ■

I remember when my mother looked at me as if she loved me.
Now she can't even look at me.

Mom was still in with Mikey. She was pushing the hair off his forehead and wiping tears off her face. I felt like crap. I was the one who should have been lying in that hospital bed, not Mikey. I did this. I was the one who wasn't there to pick him up. I was the reason why Mom couldn't stop crying. I was the loser.

"They're thinking they might bring him to a room," Mom said. She didn't look at me. I wouldn't want to look at me either. "Stay with him a minute while I go find a nurse."

She went to the other side of the curtain and I watched her feet walk away.

"Mikey?" I said.

He didn't answer. He didn't move. Maybe he was asleep.

I heard my mother talking to some nurse.

I went over to Mikey and took his hand for a second. I had something to give him. I put it in his palm and closed his fingers around it.

"I left a message on the answering machine for your father," Mom said, coming back in. "But he never checks that thing, so you should go home and tell him about Mikey."

What was I going to tell him? That his son stuffed his scotch bottles in his backpack that morning? That he tossed them up as high as he could over a big hole but one of them smashed into his head? I should tell him that?

No. That wasn't what she meant. That wasn't the family way. I was supposed to just tell him there was an accident and that Mikey was in the hospital. That was what I was supposed to say.

Why couldn't she call him back and tell him herself? Maybe she just wanted me out of there—couldn't stand my face anymore.

I nodded, and waited for a half a second to see if she was going to give me cab fare.

She didn't.

"See you later, Bugs," I said, and pushed his hand under the sheet.

It looked as if he was having a hard time keeping his fingers around that bag of M&M's I gave him.

I want my life to melt in my mouth—not in my hands.

Officer Ross was in the hospital parking lot, writing something in his notepad. "What are *you* doing here?" he asked me.

"Hey," I said, and kept walking.

"That's it? Hey? After I covered for you twice, all I get is *hey*?"

I stopped walking and shoved my hands in the front pockets of my jeans. I had no idea what the guy wanted, but whatever it was, I didn't have it to give.

"How about, Hello, Officer Ross. How are you today?"

How about, Go to hell, Officer Ross. I'm in a hurry.

"How's it going?" I asked.

"Busy day—just finished following up a call on a hit and run accident. I don't think the old guy's going to make it."

"That's hard," I said. "Listen, I got to get going. Catch ya later."

"Hold on. I told you why *I* was here. Why are *you*?"

He wasn't going to let up on me until I told him. I blew some hair off my forehead and stopped myself from rolling my eyes.

"My brother got hurt. He's in the emergency room."

He took a step over to me so we were almost toe-to-toe.

"Is he all right? What happened?"

"He was just screwing around, that's all. Hurt his head."

He squinted his eyes, then put his notepad in his pocket. "Your brother the one they picked up at the elementary school tossing bottles?"

I nodded.

"Why do you think he was doing that?"

"I don't know. Pretty stupid, huh?"

"Must have made sense to him." Ross started chewing some gum from a pack in his pocket. "Want a piece?"

My mouth was dry. That stick of gum was the first thing anybody had offered me all day. I took it.

"Where you headed? Home?"

I nodded.

"I know the way. Get in."

He walked over to his patrol car and didn't wait for me to answer him. I was too out of it to put up a fight and way too tired to walk home.

This time I got to sit in the front seat and I didn't have to wear the steel bracelets. I was just hoping he wasn't going to try and talk the whole way there.

He didn't. I was surprised. Voices blasted from his police radio and static kept crackling through the speakers. He chewed his gum and kept his eyes on the road.

He didn't say anything until we got in front of my house. He put the car in park and turned the radio down.

I looked at my house. My father's car was in the driveway.

"Maybe this thing your brother did was his way of saying something."

"I don't know," I said.

"He could have been seriously hurt. He could have killed himself if that bottle had hit him right."

I'd already thought of that.

"You don't think he wanted to hurt himself, do you?"

I shook my head.

"You've been getting into your own set of trouble lately, and I got to tell you: If you don't pull things together you're not going to be able to keep a very good eye on your brother."

"Why is that my job?"

"I bet it feels like a pretty *big* job sometimes—especially when you're doing it by yourself."

"I don't have a big brother to watch *my* back."

"Think it would make a difference for you if you did? Think maybe you wouldn't be getting as many black eyes, bad grades, scrapes with the law? Think you wouldn't be drinking or getting high?"

I stared out the window.

"All I'm saying, Pip, is that if you don't want your brother feeling like you do when *he's* sixteen, you'd better figure out a way to watch your own back and get yourself cleaned up."

I opened the car door and got out. "Thanks for the ride."

"Pip. Maybe you should put something on those hands—some antibacterial stuff or something."

I shut the car door just when he was asking me how I'd cut them.

Everybody had something to say to me. Everybody had an opinion—a vote on how I should be living my life. The noise in my head was so loud, I wanted to scream or throw something. And that noise was about to get louder.

The Grinch was standing at the door watching the cop drive away.

I want to laugh.
I think I remember how to do that.

"So what did you do now?"

He got right behind me when I walked into the house. Maybe he left an inch of space between his face and the back of my head.

"Why did a policeman bring you home?"

I didn't answer him. I didn't know what to say.

He shoved me hard in the back and I fell into the couch.

I turned around and waited for him to come at me. I didn't jump up. I didn't get ready to fight back or brace myself for a hit. I just sat there.

"Answer me. What kind of trouble you into now?"

I kept staring at him.

He swung at me, but I didn't block it. I caught a slap right in the face. My head went back a little, but I still didn't get up. I didn't move.

"Something wrong with you, boy? Get up."

I stood up in front of him, closer than he'd like. He grabbed my shirt and pushed me back against the wall.

"I'm talking to you!" he yelled. "And if you don't start answering me I'm going to clean your clock. Now tell me why you were brought home by the police."

I didn't say a word. I just stared at him. I figured I didn't owe him an answer, and I was too pissed to even talk. I didn't want to tell him a damn thing about me. I didn't even want to tell him that there wasn't anything to the ride home from the cop. Somewhere in my head I figured I deserved a beating, and I was going to stand there ready to take it.

I think it was harder for him to hit me when I wasn't putting up a fight. Maybe it wasn't as much fun for him either. He didn't slug me in the face or punch me in the stomach. He just kept slamming my back against the wall over and over again.

He was yelling about what a loser I was, that I was stupid and no damn good. I didn't feel the words any more than I felt the wall behind me. Neither one hurt.

"Get up to your room." He let go of me and walked away. "You're grounded for another week—not just for getting into trouble with the police, but for stealing my scotch off the refrigerator. Four bottles of booze gone so you and your buddies could cut school and have a party."

I took my time getting into the kitchen. I went over to the counter, turned up the volume on the answering machine, and pressed Play.

"Mike, you need to come to the hospital," my mother's voice said. "Mikey's hurt. There's been an accident."

I remember making a leaf pile with my father.

He threw me into it, and I laughed as I pulled him down with me. I got a leaf in my mouth, and Dad had a few in his hair.

We kept raking the leaves into bigger and bigger piles, and falling into them like wrestlers.

I don't think we ever got around to bagging all the leaves.
I remember it started getting dark, and all of a sudden he got up.
"Where you going?" I asked him.
"Inside," he said. "I'm thirsty."

"You know about this?" he asked me.

"Yeah."

"What happened?"

"Mikey hurt himself at school. He was playing around by a hole they're digging up there and . . . and . . ."

I wasn't sure how much I wanted to say. I didn't know how much trouble Mikey was going to be in, and I wasn't going to rat him out about the bottles.

"And he fell."

"This happened after school?"

I nodded.

"So this was your fault."

He wiped his arm across the counter, knocking everything on the floor.

"Where were you? Drinking my scotch instead of picking up your brother?"

Something in me snapped. I yelled back at him twice as loud as he yelled at me. "Where were *you*? You're never there for him. You're never there for anybody. *You're* the loser. You're the one who's supposed to take care of him, not me." I was screaming so loud I felt the words rip out of my throat like broken glass.

"Who do you think you are, talking to me like that?" He came at me but stopped a foot away.

"I don't know. Who are *you*?" I said. "You're not anybody's father. You don't know how to be a father. All you know how to do is yell and hit and drink and drink and—"

"You'd better shut your mouth."

"A father is somebody you talk to—somebody you look up to. I don't want to be like you."

"Shut your mouth!" he yelled.

"But I am. I'm *just* like you. Except for one thing."

"That's right, Pip. And that one thing is that *I* know how to take care of my responsibilities."

"Responsibilities? You don't know the first thing about it. You think having a job and paying the bills is all you're supposed to do? You think that's being a father?" I shook my head. "You don't know shit."

"I don't need to listen to this." He grabbed his car keys off the floor where he'd thrown everything.

"I'll tell you the difference between you and me," I said.

"Go to your room—"

"The difference is that my family isn't afraid of me."

He rolled his eyes. "Too bad you're afraid of yourself, Mr. Wise Guy."

He put his hand on the doorknob. "And you better hope for your sake that your brother's all right."

He slammed the door on the way out.

I wasn't sure who I hated more—him or me.

I want to write my own ending.
I'm just not sure what the story's about.

■ ■ ■

There was a brown paper bag standing on the table. I knew what it was. I knew the shape—the way the paper was scrunched closed at the top. He'd brought a bottle home before he even knew his stash was gone. Always a step ahead of his drink—that's my father.

I took the bottle out, then crunched the bag into a ball and threw it at the door.

I'd already had four joints. I figured a boost on top of it wouldn't hurt. I needed something. Everything was getting crazy. My hands were still shaking from yelling at my father, and the pictures in my head were wrestling with each other.

But there weren't just pictures in my head. There was noise. And it wasn't just any noise—it was voices. I wanted them to shut up.

Me: *All you know how to do is yell and hit and drink and drink and—*

Claire: *A lot of things don't make sense in an alcoholic family—*

Mikey: *I wanted to be like him—*

Officer Ross: *You don't want your brother feeling like you do when he's sixteen—*

Mikey: *You didn't come—*

Mom: *My poor baby—*

Dad: *So this was your fault—*

I unscrewed the cap and put the bottle to my lips. But I couldn't tip my head back. It was as if my neck was locked or something.

Kirkland: *How did this book affect you?*

Tony: *Just a punk that hangs out next to garbage and with dead people—*

Me: *I told you he wasn't going to the zoo with you—*
Mikey: *You don't know everything—*
Claire: *Bottled up—*
Kirkland: *Chances are something you don't take when you're lost—*

I took the bottle away from my lips and walked over to the sink with it. My heart was pounding, my head was hurting, and I needed to do something. I just didn't know what.

Maybe Mikey had the right idea, smashing those bottles. I could pour this one down the drain.

But somewhere in me I knew. I knew that wasn't going to change anything. My father would probably come home with another bottle before he even knew this one was gone.

I wasn't going to change him.

I wasn't sure if I would ever change myself either.

I remember my favorite song when I was a little kid.
Puff the magic dragon.
I wanted to be the boy in the song.
Instead I ended up being Puff—without the magic.

The phone rang. It was Claire.

"You're late," she said.

"For what?"

"Group. There are forty-five minutes left. You'd better get your butt here."

I put the bottle in the sink and took off. It was only a five-minute jog over to the office, but it felt as if it was a hundred miles away. With the deep hole I was digging for myself at home, the last thing I needed was Giraldi calling the house. I was lucky Claire had bothered to call me.

"Where were you?" Darius asked when I walked in.

"Something was going down at home," I said.

"What?" Paco asked.

"Nothing," I said, and Claire shot me a look.

"Pip," Claire said, "we've talked about how you hold back and—"

"I know, I know." I looked around at the guys. "My brother got hurt. He's in the hospital."

I told them pretty much the whole story. I didn't say that I'd been at the Site getting high and forgot to pick him up. But I told them I'd been late. Told them he'd hit himself in the head with one of my father's scotch bottles. That he had stuffed them in his backpack and brought them to school

"Your father drinks, huh?" Paco asked. "Like my old man?"

I nodded.

"So where were you?" Darius wanted to know. "Why were you late getting your brother?"

"I lost track of time."

"You were getting wasted," Mark said. "Look at you."

Anthony jumped in too, wanting to know how many joints I'd smoked. They were all looking at me.

"Four," I said. "Maybe when I leave here I'll have another one."

"This guy's not just wasted," Darius said. "He's a waste of time."

"Screw you. Screw all of you. I didn't ask for any of this."

"Yes, you did," Paco said. "You brought all this on."

"What are you talking about? Your father drinks," I said. "You know where I'm coming from."

"I'm all through blaming my old man for my life, Pip. Just 'cause he's a drunk, I don't have to be one. Who I am ain't his fault. Who I'm going to be is up to me."

"I don't need this crap," I said. "You all sound like you're reading scripts for a self-help play."

"So what *do* you need?" Claire asked me.

"How the hell do I know? No matter what I say, you'll tell me it's the wrong answer and that I got nothing but choices. It's a bunch of crap is what it is."

Nobody said anything for a second.

"It's getting harder to be the old you, isn't it, Pip?" she asked.

"The old me? This is who I am. This is the only me I got. It's not like I'm Jekyll and Hyde, with Jekyll waiting inside me to burst out. This is it. This is me." I hit my chest. "The only one I got. The only one I know how to be."

Darius started clapping, then Anthony joined in. Everybody was clapping, even Claire.

"What the hell are you doing that for?" I asked.

"You just unscrewed the top, and out he came," Claire said.

"Who?"

"The other you that you didn't know was in there."

I remember when I was little I used to be afraid to cross the street.

But I threw my ball into the road all the time anyway, so I could just think about what it would be like to go out there and get it.

Mom and Dad got home at about eight o'clock, and they had Mikey with them.

He was okay. At least his head was.

He was tired and quiet. I stood in his doorway watching Mom tuck him into bed, and for a second it was the old Mom, the one I remembered from when I was a kid—when I was still the cute family puppy and not the annoying mutt tied out back.

She'd tuck me into bed and pull the covers real tight around me so I'd stay warm. Then she'd tell me a story, tickle me under my arms or joke about my smelly feet. If I was sick she'd have this look on her face that said if anything ever happened to me she wouldn't be able to keep living. It was a face that said she'd do anything to keep me safe. It said she loved me.

She had that look on her face while she was getting Mikey into bed. But it didn't stick around long. Neither did she.

"Stay with him 'til he's asleep," she said, walking out of the room.

She looked tired. Her eyes were half closed. That could have been either because she was wiped out or because she'd taken one of her Valiums.

Or it could have just been because she was sad. Being sad all the time might make a person look real tired.

My mother looked friggin' exhausted.

I walked over to Mikey's bed and sat next to him. Bugs Bunny was on the floor. I picked it up and put it under his blanket where he could get it. He didn't move, and his eyes were closed.

"You okay, Bugs? How you feeling?"

He didn't answer. I figured the kid was real mad at me for not picking him up. He'd found out what a shit I was and how bad I'd been letting him down. He was just getting his energy together so he could tell me off.

I waited for it. I had it coming.

Tears started coming down his cheeks. First one, then two, then like seven or eight.

"What's the matter? You hurting?"

He nodded.

"Your head hurts? I'll get Mom."

He shook his head.

"What's wrong? Why are you crying?"

He swallowed, and then said, "I'm sorry."

If words could kill I would have been dead on the spot.

"What the hell are *you* sorry for?"

He still didn't open his eyes.

"I'm in big trouble, right?"

"For what, Mikey?"

"I broke Daddy's bottles. The police came."

"The police didn't come because you busted the bottles. They came because you got hurt."

"Am I going to jail?"

"No, of course not."

"Are *you* going to jail?"

He was crying so hard, I could hardly hear the question.

"Why would you think that?"

"I saw the policeman bring you home that night. I looked outside and I saw him."

It *had* been my brother at the window. That's probably why he'd gone and hid in the closet with that bottle.

So that was my fault too.

"Nobody's going to jail," I told him.

"I'm sorry, Pip. I'm sorry I do wrong things."

I put my hand under his head and gently pulled him against my chest.

"You're not the one that should be sorry," I said.

"I'm the one who broke the bottles."

I didn't know how to explain it to him, and I sure wasn't as good at apologizing as he was.

"Maybe there shouldn't have been any bottles to break," I said.

He wiped his nose on the bottom of my shirt.

"What do you mean?"

"I mean how about not wiping your snot on me."

He almost smiled, and that was good enough for me. I'd thought he forgot how.

"Pip?"

"Yeah."

"How do they know how many M&M's to put in the bags? Like how many red ones and how many green ones—how do they know?"

"You're supposed to be asleep."

"Pip?"

"What?"

"I got a headache," he said.

"Yeah." I gave his pillow a hit, and he lay back down on it. "I bet you got one hell of a headache."

I want to learn how to take pictures.

The kind you take with a camera. Not the kind my head takes.

My head uses real expensive film and the pictures are a bitch to develop.

I woke up shaking from a nightmare.

I dreamt I was at the Site. Mikey was following me, and I was trying to outrun him but couldn't.

I got to Beattie's headstone and lit a joint, hoping Mikey wouldn't catch up with me and see me getting high. I took a deep drag and closed my eyes for just a second.

When I opened them and blew out the smoke, Mikey was sitting on the grass leaning against Agnes. He was rolling his own joint.

"What are you running from me for?" he asked. "I'm faster than you."

He lit the joint and sucked in hard, smiling the whole time. I went to pull the joint out of his mouth, but slipped. I fell back and whacked my head on the headstone.

"That had to hurt," Mikey said, still smoking away.

I rubbed my head and turned around to see what I'd knocked into. I jumped up when I saw it.

The headstone didn't say Beattie.

It said Downs.

Phillip Downs.

I want a joint so the bones in my hands will stop shaking under my skin.

That's what I need—new joints.

Mom stayed home with Mikey. I was surprised, but I guess I wasn't supposed to be. She's his mother. I just had the feeling she was going to ask *me* to do it. It would have been better than going to classes anyway.

Maybe she needed the day off. She'd been up most of the night listening to the Grinch yell at her. He'd been yelling that what happened to Mikey was her fault—that she was a lousy mother and she was lazy and she was stupid and on and on and on.

She didn't yell back, but I heard her crying.

I stayed in my room. It wasn't up to me to run down there and get in the middle of it.

Like Claire says, we all have choices and Mom made hers by staying with him.

I felt bad for her, though. Some choices are hard. Change is hard. I sure knew that. Sometimes just doing what you've always known is a lot easier than trying to do something different.

Mom was standing at the sink rinsing out her coffee mug when I went through the kitchen on my way to school. I wanted to say something, but I didn't know what. I'm not a big word guy. I could yell at my parents pretty good. I just didn't know how to talk to them.

"See you later," I said.

It was the best I could do.

I want what I want, and I want it to get here faster.

Coach Fredericks picked me first for this crazy obstacle course he'd set up. I couldn't climb up to the top of the rope. I fell on my ass twice.

"Got to clear out those smoked-up lungs, Mr. Downs," he said.

Bend over so I can blow it out your—

Every teacher that day got on my case about something.

One good thing happened, though. Jenna nabbed me after

Kirkland's class and said she was treating me to lunch. How could I say no? She smiled at me *and* she was buying.

The only cafeteria food that won't kill you is the chicken fingers. We both got that, fries, and soda. We took our trays to the back near where the freshmen eat, so nobody from any of our classes would come over and get in our way.

"Thanks for having lunch with me," she said.

"Why'd you want to? We don't hang out together or anything."

"We're hanging out now."

She smiled. I took a bite of a chicken finger because I felt my face getting hot.

I wasn't sure how to talk to a girl—especially to a girl I liked. Not being at least a little stoned made it even harder.

"I don't think it's right for you to treat me like I have a disease," she said. "Just because I go to counseling."

"What?"

"You've been acting as if you don't know me ever since you saw me at the counseling center."

"That's not because I saw you there. It's because . . ."

"Because what?"

"Because you saw *me* there."

"That's crazy."

"It wasn't crazy when *you* were thinking it."

She laughed. "I'll show you mine if you show me yours."

"What are you talking about?"

"You tell me why you go, and I'll tell you why I do."

"You first," I said, figuring it would give me time to come up with a good story.

"Fine." She took a deep breath, then started talking. There

were three kids in her family, she told me. She was the middle kid and she had a younger sister. She used to have an older brother—until two years ago.

"When he died I got left holding the bag. My parents were too screwed up over Rick's death to be parents anymore, so I had to take care of my little sister."

"How'd he die?"

She took a sip of her soda and waited as if she was trying to decide how much to say.

"First tell me why *you're* in counseling?"

"Okay." I cleared my throat. "Giraldi said if I didn't go he was going to expel me."

"Why counseling? Why not detention for the year, or community service?"

"He thought I needed someone to talk to."

"Do you?"

I shrugged.

"So," I said, "how did your brother die?"

"He overdosed on pills," she said without skipping a beat.

"He killed himself?"

"We're not sure, but the story is that he partied too much one night. There was no note and he had a lot of booze in him."

"Shit," was all I could say.

"Got that right. I really miss him sometimes." She looked away for a second, then down at her food. "Ever since he died I'm the mommy, the daddy, and the big sister all wrapped up in one teenager."

"I take care of my little brother a lot too. I don't think I'm as good at it as you probably are with your sister—"

"How do you know that?"

"Trust me. I've been screwing up a lot lately."

"How?"

"I don't know . . ."

"Yes, you do. Tell me one thing you did to screw up."

"Okay. My father was supposed to go on this zoo trip with him, and he finked out at the last second. I dragged Mikey to school and made him get on the bus and go when it was the last thing he wanted to do." I shook my head. "The kid was probably embarrassed the old man didn't come through for him."

"So how did you screw up? What do you *wish* you'd done?"

I took a drink of soda and thought for a second about whether I wanted to answer.

"I wish I had just bagged school and gotten on the bus with him."

She nodded. "Well, maybe one day I'll get my sister and the four of us can take our own trip to the zoo."

"Sounds good," I said, taking a bite of chicken. "So how do you screw up with your sister?"

"Last week I gave her pizza for dinner."

"So? I eat pizza all the time."

"It was frozen pizza."

"I eat those too. They're great."

"I forgot to cook it."

I laughed. "You gave her *frozen* frozen pizza?"

"*She* didn't think it was funny," Jenna said, laughing with me.

I put my hand on my cheek.

"What's wrong?" she asked.

"Nothing," I said. "It's stupid."

"No, it isn't. Eating frozen pizza is stupid. Tell me."

"My face just hurt for a second."

"From the black eye you got last week?"

"No, because I haven't laughed or smiled in a while. It's like my face wasn't used to it, so it hurt."

She stared at me with a goofy smile on her face.

"I told you it was stupid," I said. "You can't believe I'd say something so dumb. Right?"

"No." She shook her head. "But now it's my turn to sound corny—"

"Oh, so I sounded corny?"

"Maybe a little. But I was just going to say something about how you act so tough. You have such a mean face and try to act like such a badass, but you're really just a mush."

"What are you talking about?"

"You're hard on the outside but really sweet on the inside. You're like, I don't know, you're like an M&M or something."

That was funnier than she'd ever know.

I want everything to stop feeling crazy. I want to stop feeling crazy.

Mom was in Mikey's room with him when I got home. It looked as if they'd spent the whole day in there.

"Tell her to let me out," Mikey begged me.

"He's been in his room all day?" I asked my mother.

"He has to be careful," she said.

"He can't hide in here forever."

"Just to the living room," Mikey said, putting his hands together as if he was praying. "Puh-leeeese."

"Tell you what." She got off his bed and stretched her back. "I need a few things from the store for dinner. You keep him out of trouble while I'm gone," she said to me. "But when I come home, he's going right back to bed to rest until it's time to eat."

Mikey waited for her to get down the stairs before he jumped off the bed and opened his closet.

"Want to play Superman with me?" He took a handful of action figures out of a box and held them up.

"Bring them downstairs," I said. "We'll put the TV on and hang out."

Downstairs Mikey jacked up the volume on the TV while I went into the kitchen to ask my mother to get me some of those peanut butter granola bars I liked. She was standing at the sink, and just when I walked in I saw her tossing a pill into her throat and chasing it back with a glass of water. It was one thing to think about my mother popping pills. It was something else to see her do it for real.

I think it hit me right then. I wasn't just my father's son. I was my mother's too.

"What are you doing, Mom?"

She pushed the pill bottle into her purse and wiped her lips. "I'm getting ready to go. Keep a good eye on your brother. He can't do a lot of jumping around, and if he says he feels dizzy—"

"Mom." I reached right into her pocketbook and took out the bottle. "What do you need these for?"

She grabbed it back, put it in her purse, and zipped it shut.

"My doctor gave them to me," she said.

"Why?"

"Pip, I'm leaving for the store. I don't have to stand here and answer to you."

"It was okay for you to get on me about what kind of brother I am. What kind of mother are *you*, wasted on pills?"

"You don't know what you're talking about. Those might be the only thing making it possible for me to get up in the morning—"

"It's not easy for anybody to get up in the mornings around here—"

"Life is no picnic for me these days—"

"I know—"

"You don't know. You have no idea what it's like being married to an alcoholic—"

"I have to watch it played out every day."

But then we both stopped.

Alcoholic.

Nobody had ever said that in our house. The shock of her saying it was hitting both of us right between our words.

"Listen," she said in a quieter voice. "I've got one son on his way to being no better than his drunken father—"

Thanks, Mom.

"—and another son who needs a lot more than I can give him—who I am basically raising alone."

"You're not raising him alone."

She shook her head as if she thought I was stupid or crazy. "I'm going to the store," she said.

"Who do you think walks him to school and back?" I asked her. "Who takes him to T-ball? Who answers all his dumb questions? Who holds him at night when you and Dad are screaming downstairs?"

I didn't mean to make her cry.

It just busted out of her like a bullet, and then she pushed past me to get outside.

"Mom?" I ran out the door after her.

"Get inside and take care of Mikey. You think I'm such a

horrible mother, maybe you should start picking up the slack and be a better brother."

She got in her car and slammed the door.

I didn't try to stop her from driving off. I let her go.

I wasn't sure why she'd gotten so upset. I didn't say anything different from what she had said to me in Mikey's room that day I yelled at him for eating my pot.

I guess it just sounded different when it was being aimed at her.

I remember one time when I was about six and my mom was real sick. She had a puking thing and couldn't hold her head up.

I brought her Jell-O, chicken soup, ginger ale. Everything she ate or drank came back up.

I got smart and stopped bringing her food.

Instead I got my pillow and some comic books, and I brought her me.

When Mom got home she sent Mikey back up to his room.

I was still feeling bad about making her cry. I carried in the grocery bags and even tried to put some of the stuff away for her.

I opened a box of peanut butter granola bars—the ones I'd never got around to asking her to pick up. She'd bought them for me anyway.

I took a bite, then said, "Mom, I didn't mean to make you cry before. I—"

"Let's not talk about it," she said without even looking at me.

I knew how to do that. We all knew how in my house. Things happen and then we all pretend they didn't.

"Mom? Can I show you something?"

"What?"

"In the living room. I want to show you something I did."

She followed me into the living room, and I brought her over to the bookshelves. Her eyes teared up again. No matter what I did I made my mother cry.

"Where'd you find these?" she asked, picking up one of the statues.

"They were in the garage. I thought they'd look better inside."

She didn't look up at me, but she put a hand on the back of my neck and gave it a squeeze.

"So what do you call these statues anyway?" I asked her.

"Precious Moments," she said. I could hear her smiling.

It was one of those warm fuzzy times. Just the thing a guy like me gets away from as fast as he can.

"I'm going to make sure Mikey's back in bed," I said.

She nodded and put the statue back on the shelf.

It was a weird-looking thing—a little boy with a very big head, sitting on a stool and wearing a dunce cap.

I want a map that'll show me how to get to all the places I haven't thought of yet.

No, I don't.

I want to leave it all to chance.

I waited until I saw Mikey go inside the building—just in case.

The construction crew was outside filling up the hole. I guess they were finally done fixing whatever was broken down there.

There was a pass from Giraldi waiting for me in first period. He wanted me to go right to his office.

"I didn't do anything," I said when I got there.

"Good morning to you too." He shut the door behind me. "Have a seat."

I flopped into my chair and let my laces slap as hard as they could on the floor.

"Any thoughts on getting a haircut?" he asked.

"Any thoughts on getting a face-lift?"

He sat down at his desk and opened up my file. He loves doing that.

"So you've been doing a pretty good job of staying out of my office—"

"You sent me a pass because you missed me so much? You could have got us some bagels and coffee."

"I don't miss you, Phillip."

"Pip."

"I don't miss you one bit. I just wanted us to check in with each other—I wanted to be sure you still understood the rules. If you go to counseling and make it to all your classes, you get to stay in school and no phone call goes home."

"I remember."

"Have you heard from your partners in crime? John or Frank?"

"I thought you said Johnny got time and Slayer was sent to rehab."

"That's true. I thought they might have written you or called."

I shook my head. I started wondering why they hadn't.

"It's probably better for you this way—easier to clean yourself up."

"Is that what I'm doing?"

"What would you call it?"

"Being blackmailed."

He closed my file and stood up. "Okay," he said. "Go back to class."

"That's it? That's all you wanted?"

"You don't make problems for *me*, I don't make any for *you*. See how this works?"

I went to the door and was almost home free.

"Downs," he said, smiling. "Keep up the good work."

He had to ruin everything.

I want some stronger kryptonite.
But I'll probably have to make it myself.

I was waiting for Mikey when he got out of school.

As soon as we started walking home, he went right into his thing.

"Pip?"

"What?"

"Why do M&M's taste so good?"

"Candy tastes good."

"I don't like Baby Ruth bars—too many nuts."

"I don't like nuts either."

"Pip?"

"What?"

"How come you have hair under your arms?"

"Mikey, shut up."

He did for about half a minute.

"Pip? Do you have to see that lady today? The one we talked to?"

"Yeah. Why?"

"I want to see her too. She was nice."

"You want to talk to her?"

"Yeah. Can I come in with you again?"

"No."

He looked as if I'd I kicked him.

"But maybe she can hook you up with somebody else to talk to when I go." I couldn't believe I was saying that. "It's not a bad idea. This way you're not in the waiting room just waiting."

"But that's what waiting rooms are for," he said.

"Don't you ever get sick of waiting, Bugs?"

"Yup," he said, and blew some hair off his forehead.

He came with me to Claire's and waited on the couch. I brought my cigarettes and matches in with me.

I told Claire he wanted to talk to somebody. She didn't look surprised. I think she was even trying not to smile. She said there was another counselor he could see while I was in with her. She ran some Kids Are People group for children of alcoholics. Claire was going to set it all up.

"Things getting any easier for you?" Claire asked me.

"No. They suck. Things are getting harder."

"Changing from who you think you have to be into who you're meant to be is one of the biggest challenges you'll ever face."

"Do you always talk in bumper stickers?"

"Do you always turn into a wiseass when things get uncomfortable?"

I nodded.

"Then I'm always going to talk in bumper stickers," she said.

"Maybe you wrote the one I saw this morning."

"What did it say?"

"I'm not telling."

"Of course you're not."

"You're always asking me what I want, and I finally figured it out from a bumper sticker on the back of some whacko's car."

"But you're still not going to tell me what it said?"

"First tell me why you don't have a clock in here."

"Who said I don't?" She swiveled back and forth in her chair.

"You have a clock in here? Where?"

She pointed behind me. There was a digital clock half the size of a dollar with huge red numbers. It was stuck to the leg of the coffee table under the window. I couldn't believe I'd missed it.

"That's cold," I said. "You're as bad as anybody in group."

"I'm not trying to be sneaky, Pip. The people who come to see me have enough to worry about. They don't need to be concerned about what time it is too. I keep track of when the sessions start and end."

"Why didn't you just tell me you had a clock when I was asking you about it?"

"You never asked me if I had a clock. You asked me why I didn't have a clock."

"That's messed up," I said.

"Is your urine going to be?" She handed me a cup.

"No way. This one is going to be a vanilla milkshake."

"Good," she said. "I'm thirsty."

"That's sick," I said.

"You can dish it out, but you can't take it."

"Got that right."

■ ■ ■

I remember when I thought I had all the answers.
I remember lying to myself.

"You throwing up?" Mikey asked me while I was bending over the bowl.

"No. Not throwing up—throwing out."

"Oh, that stuff," he said. "I didn't like how it tasted anyway."

"Good," I said, flushing what I had left of the two bags Johnny had given me.

He took my pack of rolling papers off the floor. "What's this?" he asked.

"That's for making paper airplanes," I told him.

We sat on the bathroom floor and made about twelve of them.

They flew pretty good—pretty high too.

I remember too much.
I think it'll get better, though. I found a place that has pretty big photo albums.

My father was sitting at the kitchen table, rattling ice cubes in his glass. Mom was putting Mikey to bed and I was walking around the house like a lion in a cage.

I couldn't stand being grounded anymore. It was hard enough getting to all my classes, and it was more than killing me not being able to get high like I used to. I had to at least figure out a way to get some cash and get off being grounded.

I sat down at the table across from my father. He looked

tired—just like Mom. It made me think about Mikey saying he thought Dad drank because he was sad.

"What is it?" he said, finishing off his drink.

"I wanted to ask you about not being grounded anymore."

"After all the crap you've been pulling?"

"I want to get some driving lessons."

I pulled the bottle cap out of my pocket and started spinning it on the table. It gave me something to look at instead of him.

"Driving lessons?" He rattled the ice cubes some more. "I told you you're not responsible enough to be on the road."

"I need fifty dollars for my first lesson."

"You're not listening to me, are you?"

I kept spinning the cap.

"You're a piece of work," he said.

"I figure if I had a license I could get a job, drive to work, be responsible."

"What do you know about being responsible?"

"I could save money and buy a car."

"A car?"

"Sure. I could park it in the garage since it's clean now. You're not using it."

He looked at me and for a second I looked back. I wasn't sure how much he remembered about that night he chased me and Mikey into the garage. I didn't even know if he ever figured out that he was the one who gave me the black eye.

"I should wait as long to take you off of being grounded as it took *you* to clean that garage."

"I don't know why I had to clean it anyway. It wasn't my mess."

"Pour me another drink," he said. He pushed his glass across the table.

I kept spinning the cap. I didn't want to fix him a drink. I didn't want a father who drank like him, and I didn't want to help him do it.

"I'm not pouring any drinks these days," I told him.

He snorted and got up from the table. "You're drinking straight from the bottle now?"

"I'm not like you," I said.

That just slipped out of my mouth, as if the words had been hanging on my lips for weeks.

I heard the scotch splash into his glass, then the sound of the bottle being slid back onto the top of the fridge.

He came back over to the table and sat down. "No. You're not like me."

He took a drink, and then put his glass on the table and started twisting it around in circles. I was still spinning the bottle cap. I don't think we were able to look at each other.

"I'm a man who's angry most of the time and sorry the rest of it," he said. "You're just angry."

I stopped spinning the cap. "I never heard you say you were sorry."

"You're more like my father than you are like me," he said, totally ignoring my last comeback. I let it go because he was talking about his old man. I don't remember my grandfather. He died when I was three years old. My father never said too much about him.

"He was an angry, angry man. I don't think I ever saw him smile. Not even on Christmas."

He took a long pull from his glass. "I never liked him," he said, then looked right at me. He kept his eyes on mine for like a million years. At least it felt that long.

"Your father teach *you* how to drive?" It was all I could think to say to get him to stop staring at me. And I guess I wanted to know too.

"I took public transportation until I was twenty-two. A man I worked with named Bud Oleman taught me how to drive."

He took another drink.

"My father never taught me how to ride a bike either. Uncle Freddy did that one Sunday on my cousin Jack's three-speed Raleigh."

"Did you ever tell him how much you hated him?"

"No. I didn't want to hurt him."

"Why not?"

"I loved him like hell," he said. He took another drink and held on to the glass. "He was my father."

He threw his head back to finish off his drink.

"Ball game's on," he said, then got up from the table and brought his glass to the counter for a refill. He didn't move when he got there. He just stood at the counter, staring out the window.

I went over, took something out of my pocket, and put it on the counter where he could see it.

"I found this in the garage," I said.

He picked it up, and for a split second I caught his smile

"Seems like a whole other life ago," he said with his eyes still on the picture. "You were angry at me that day too—couldn't understand why I had to let go of the back of the bike."

He put the picture on the counter and went back to looking out the window.

"Couldn't understand why I had to let go," he said again, shaking his head. "Anyway. I don't want to miss the game." He dumped his ice cubes in the sink and opened the freezer for some fresh ones.

I started to walk out of the kitchen, but he called me back.

"Don't forget this," he said.

I turned around, figuring he was going to give me back the picture, but he had a fifty-dollar bill in his hand.

"For the driving lesson," he said.

I took the fifty from him, and he turned around fast. The picture wasn't on the counter anymore and I didn't ask for it back. I had another copy where all the other pictures in my head were.

We didn't say anything else. Maybe there wasn't anything else to say.

I went outside and he didn't stop me, so I figured I wasn't grounded anymore.

I was free, but I didn't really have anyplace to go. All my friends were either dead or on their way to being dead.

I could hear the ice cubes cracking out of their tray in the kitchen.

I took what I was holding in my hand and threw it across the street as far as I could.

It felt a lot heavier than just a bottle cap.

But it went pretty far.

I know what I want.

I finally figured it out.

A car went by the other day, and I caught a look at one of the bumper stickers plastered on the back.

All the things I thought I wanted really come down to the same thing.

Peace.

I do know what I want. I just haven't been saying it right.

But now that I know, I have to figure out how I'm ever going to find it.

So I've been sitting in the driveway thinking about everything. Sort of playing the whole story out in my head. I thought it all started when Fleming "had it with me" and made me go to Giraldi's office. Now I'm thinking it started way before that. It started sometime I'll never be able to really put my finger on.

I think change is something that starts out small, before you notice it. Then out of nowhere it kicks you in the ass and makes you pay attention.

Mikey's been running up and down this driveway for over an hour, shooting hoops. He keeps trying to get me to play with him, but I haven't played ball since I was a kid. It's not a part of who I am anymore. I hope *he* keeps playing, though. Like the doctor said, I'd rather see him throwing balls than bottles.

"You're a chicken," he says, starting up with me again.

"What are you talking about?"

"You're too scared to play me because I'm better than you."

"I don't like basketball."

"Dad put this hoop up for *you.*"

"Yeah, back when I was young and stupid like you."

"Chicken," he says, and takes a shot.

"Why do you want me to play ball with you?"

"We got nothing else to do. All you been doing is just sitting there smoking cigarettes."

"You can go to Eddie's house if you want."

"No thanks."

"Why not?"

"I'd rather hang out with you."

"What for? I'm boring."

"You're super boring. I just want to, that's all."

He's dribbling the ball right by me, so I hit it out of his hand.

"Hey," he yells.

"Hay is for horses," I say, and dribble the ball down to the end of the driveway.

My brother's looking at me as if he's seeing a ghost. But he's smiling.

He runs down the driveway and tries to get the ball from me. He comes close a few times but I'm too fast for him.

"I thought you were supposed to be good at this," I say.

"Time out," he yells, then bends over to tie his sneakers.

"Time out," I tease him. "You're just too chicken to play me."

"I'll show you," he says, taking his time looping his lace around to make a knot.

"Pip?"

I stop dribbling, because my lungs are used to smoke—not exercise.

"How come M&M's are soft on the inside and hard on the outside?"

While I'm coughing I'm thinking about what Jenna said to me about being that way.

"Because," I tell him, "that's just the way it is with M&M's."

I go back to dribbling, and he comes after me. I turn to the left, then to the right. I'm about to take another shot, but I almost trip.

Mikey yells again. "Time out!"

"Now what?" I say with the ball under my arm.

He walks over and squats down in front of me. He pulls my laces hard and starts tying my shoes.

And I let him.

I'm not going to be anybody's hero. He can do stuff for me sometimes too, like wake me up from myself.

And I can get my ass to counseling and try to stay clean and sober so I don't forget to pick him up anymore—so I can keep an eye on him.

I can try that.

For now I'll do it for him. Someday, if it catches on, I'll do it for myself.

But me and Bugs—we're going to get our slice of the pizza, our piece of the pie. Our peace.

And it's all going to start right here in the driveway, running around shooting hoops—both of us with red capes flying off the backs of our shirts.

ACKNOWLEDGMENTS

So many people to thank for so many reasons . . .

Laura Heisler—for time, for space, for trying, for giving

Emma—for her hugs after long writing sessions—for understanding about dreams

Lucky—for being a tye-dyed spirit and Mommy's little Buddha

Regina Abdou—for helping me cough up the very first pages—my throat still hurts

Jason Coffman—for being my escort, my cheerleader, and my best friend

John Murray, Jr.—for teaching me how to look beyond the obvious—that really helps writing

Marie Murray—for helping me develop a passion for books

Debbie Whitman—for showing up just in time to watch the dream wake me up

Christine Pellicano—for being the first to tell me to go for it

Wendy Baker—for her enthusiasm and for always watching my literary back

Gertrude—for giving me a lot to think about

Shihan Chris Colombo—for providing a safe outlet for demon slaying

Connie Newman—for reality checks when reality was the last priority

Lisa Hollinger Sorensen—for turning graveyard smiles into a Kodak moment

Lauri Hornik—for taking a chance—for easing me into all of this with such care and consideration

■ ■ ■

Every project has a soundtrack. I am grateful to all the music that kept me company as this story unfolded again and again. To name a few:

> "Superman" by Five for Fighting; "Evaporated" by Ben Folds Five; "Dragon Attack" by Queen (RAK and Jack Benson remix); "The More We Try" by Kenny Loggins; "Downed" by Cheap Trick; "Ooh Child" by Valerie Carter; "Never Surrender" by Corey Hart; "Jump" by Kris Kross; "Any Lucky Penny" by Nikki Hessman; "Where We Were Before" by Blessed Union of Souls; "Out of My Head" by Fastball; "Down Boys" by the Cars; "Family Portrait" by Pink; "Speak Now or Forever Hold Your Peace" by Cheap Trick

A special thanks to all the kids and teens who shared their stories with me during our time together at Daytop Village, ADAPP, and the Harrison Youth Council.